SONGS FROM THE DEPTHS

MEG SWANSON

Halo
PUBLISHING
INTERNATIONAL

Halo Publishing International
7550 WIH-10 #800, PMB 2069,
San Antonio, TX 78229

First Edition, May 2023
ISBN: 978-1-63765-372-2
Library of Congress Control Number: 2023901391

Halo Publishing International is a self-publishing company that publishes adult fiction and non-fiction, children's literature, self-help, spiritual, and faith-based books. We continually strive to help authors reach their publishing goals and provide many different services that help them do so. We do not publish books that are deemed to be politically, religiously, or socially disrespectful, or books that are sexually provocative, including erotica. Halo reserves the right to refuse publication of any manuscript if it is deemed not to be in line with our principles. Do you have a book idea you would like us to consider publishing? Please visit www.halopublishing.com for more information.

Author's Note

This novel takes place on an Earth where magic and mythical creatures exist. While I have pulled elements from my favorite mythologies and folklore, this is not meant to be an accurate representation of the source material.

In loving memory of Phyllis Dobrin,
who knew I could do it before I did.

To my husband, Matt, who ran with all my
wild ideas and supported all of my insane
ramblings until we got here. I love you.

Thank you to my Beta Crew! You all
are amazing, and I am so lucky to
have you in my life!

Next, where the Sirens dwells, you plough the seas;
Their song is death, and makes destruction please.
Unblest the man whom music wins to stay
Nigh the cursed shore and listen to the lay.

. . . .

In verdant meads they sport; and wide around
Lie human bones that whiten all the ground:
The ground polluted floats with human gore,
And human carnage taints the dreadful shore.

—Homer, Odyssey

CONTENTS

Part Three

Part IV

Prologue

The morning sun sliced across her eyelids. Reluctantly, she opened them. Bones clattered as wings the color of the new moon stretched beyond the Siren's fingertips. She stood and walked to the mouth of the cave, glaring out at the glistening lake. She raked ragged claws through masses of tangled, gritty hair. Thea inhaled deeply, and a cruel smile smoothed the irritation from her face. The air carried the bright, sharp tang of magic. "Ah, finally." She strode toward the lake's edge and, with an ear-piercing shriek, leapt into the air. Wings outstretched, the Siren barrel-rolled and angled herself toward the mirrorlike surface.

*

The bell jingled above the door. Gus looked up from his newspaper in dismay; another group of campers had vanished without a trace. Gus had begun tracking the disappearances when they first started happening on the East Coast. He had hoped, foolishly, that when they stopped, whatever had been hunting those poor people would have been caught. Yet, here he was, six months later, reading about more people vanishing. This time, though, they were disappearing in his backyard. Gus knew that these disappearances weren't going to stop until whatever was taking these people found what it was hunting.

A group of twentysomethings barreled in laughing and jostling each other. Gus scrubbed his hands over his face; he had to stop following the news so closely. People went missing every day, and these campers and through hikers were no different. *But there are just so many of them now,* Gus thought, worried that every customer who came in would be the next one to disappear.

"Uh, excuse me? Do you have any Pop-Tarts?"

Gus stood and limped over to the side of the counter. He pointed in the direction of the appropriate aisle and said, "The far aisle over there has all the supplies I carry for through hikers. If you're going to get Pop-Tarts, you might also want to grab a few of the vacuum-sealed tuna packets. They're shelf stable, have protein, and I hear are a great snack for long hiking days."

A girl with black, curly hair exploding around a bright-blue bandana smiled, turned to someone who seemed to hardly exist on this plane, and pointed.

Gus looked behind the first two and watched the boys with them grab as much Gatorade as they could hold. "You might want to trade some of those out for water. Nothing beats actual hydration."

The smaller of the boys turned to Gus and smiled. "I've been trying to tell him that, but he won't listen."

"Oh, Ryan! I didn't realize it was you." Gus's wan smile turned warm as he realized that this group of kids had an experienced hiker with them.

"Heya, Gus. Don't worry. I'll make sure we have all the right gear."

Gus held up his hand in a gesture of mock surrender and chuckled. He limped back to his stool behind the counter. "I'll let you kids be. I'm here if you have any other questions." He sat down heavily.

This crew would be safe from whatever was out there. Ryan had been camping on this section of trail since he could walk. His parents used to bring him every summer, and when he was old enough, he had started coming out here by himself almost every weekend in the spring and summer.

The girl he had spoken to earlier walked up to the cash register while her friends all went out to the bright-orange Jeep waiting outside. She had an armload of snacks, matches, and duct tape.

"Is this all you need, then? You have all you need for your protection spell?"

She smiled broadly as she pulled out her wallet. "We're not using magic. Your buddy Ryan is taking us to where he always camps. He says it's within walking distance of a rangers' station and not too far off of the main trail."

Gus nodded, feeling some of the concern return, but he ignored it. "Well. Be safe out there."

The girl nodded back, and her neon-blue bandana slid farther down her hair. "We will. Thanks!"

Gus watched as she bounded out the door and ran to her friends. He looked back down at the photograph of the latest abandoned campsite. Gus closed his eyes, lit the bark that had fallen from his arm earlier, and sent a prayer into the universe that the young people would be safe and protected. The bell jingled again, and Gus smiled at the beautiful woman who glided in, promptly forgetting Ryan and his friends before the flame went out.

PART ONE

THE STORYKEEPER

Inscribed on the skin,
Yet invisible to the naked eye
Lie the Stories.
The uplifting honor,
And
The crushing responsibility.
Blurry visions flit across
The minds' eye. Taking first
The mind of the StoryKeeper
And eventually
Their life.

John

I smiled at Marissa as she ran out of the convenience store. She climbed into the driver's seat and turned to Ryan, who was sitting in the back. "Ry, that guy in there is weird."

I pushed myself off the side of the Jeep, grabbed the passenger seat, and pushed it forward to climb into the back.

"Ow! Watch it, John!"

I let go of the seat, and it dropped back into place with Nova in it. "Wow! I am so sorry. I didn't even see you there."

"Yeah"—Nova grimaced—"I get that a lot."

I shrugged and climbed into the back, over Nova; we had been friends for years, ever since Ryan had introduced them to us, and to this day, it was always a shock to me when Nova just appeared, seemingly out of thin air. No one ever talked about Nova's magic, and we didn't bring it up. It was obviously a sore subject for them, so we all just accepted it. I settled back and tore open my bag of chips, wondering why no one was sitting shotgun. Ryan leaned forward through the center console and gave Marissa instructions to where we were headed. As Ryan seemed to have this whole trip handled, I sank into the gentle bumping and rocking of the Jeep and let my eyes close.

*

I woke up in a small apartment that I didn't recognize. I whirled, looking for something, anything, that I recognized. Where was I?

A creak behind me, and the door opened. A woman with long brown hair stepped inside. I narrowed my eyes. There was definitely something familiar about her. I shook my head and grimaced at her. "Who are you?" She didn't acknowledge me at all. "Hello?" Nothing. The woman went about her routine of dropping her keys in a bowl on a table, hanging up her jacket, and dropping her purse on the floor. "Can you hear me? I am not supposed to be here."

Still nothing.

Dammit. What was happening?

"Nan?" A deep female voice called.

I whipped my head around. Nan?

The woman in front of me smiled and took off her coke-bottle sunglasses. "No. I'm a big, nasty, monstrous robber. This is a stickup!"

A gravelly laugh followed a cloud of smoke, which obscured the face of a smallish woman with lank blonde hair. "Oh good. I was getting bored."

Nan laughed, and suddenly everything became clear. I could feel the tattoo on the back of my hand burn. It was happening already. The stories were coming.

*

"John!"

I jerked awake. The Jeep was parked, and my friends were all staring at me. "What? Are we here?"

Ryan covered my left hand and looked worriedly into my eyes. He breathed in deeply and exhaled slowly. And again.

I felt myself matching Ryan's breathing. The burning on my hand subsided, and I felt more grounded.

Ryan shook out his hand as though he had been burned. "Yes. We're here."

I nodded, trying to act as though everything were totally normal. "Then let's go!"

I leapt out of the Jeep with more confidence than I actually felt. Ryan started unloading the packs, and I took a deep breath. Yes. This was the best way to say goodbye. I turned and watched my friends bicker about whose pack was heavier. Ryan laughed gently and put his hand out to the empty— *No, wait, Nova is there.*

I smiled, concentrating on this moment, committing it to memory. My heart rune warmed my chest, causing my eyes to water. Whoever inherited my Stories would get this one; I could only hope that they were able to feel the love and not the sadness I had at leaving them all behind.

*

Ryan led us along the trail, and every so often he stopped, briefly consulted the map and his compass, and then took off in an unexpected direction. Every time we did this, the trail narrowed until we were barely on a footpath. "Dude, where is this place?"

Ryan smiled and looked back at his compass. Then he frowned.

Marissa and Nova turned; Marissa fisted her hands on her hips, and Nova stepped up to see what Ryan was looking at.

"Ry, what's up?"

"My compass. It's spinning."

"Well? What does that mean?" Marissa asked impatiently.

Ryan shrugged and dropped the compass back in his pocket. "It means, thank gods, we're close, because there has been some sort of weird magnetic shift."

Marissa looked at me with worry creasing her brow and then back at Ryan. "You're sure you know what you're doing?"

Ryan looked up from his map. "I sure do." He started to fold it back up as precisely as it had looked when he bought it. "As long as we keep that water tower in front of us, we should be at the site by nightfall."

We all turned in the direction that Ryan was pointing and barely saw the top of a water tower.

Nova gripped Ryan's arm and briefly shimmered. "Famous last words, man."

*

It was getting dark. We were all tense, tired, and terse. I smiled at my alliteration; it had been one of Zelda's favorite games to break hard silences. She would nudge me in the back seat, point out the window, and say, "Traffic, time, Toods."

Toods—the tattoo on my left hand warmed again, this time gently. I didn't often think of my sister, but it felt as though I needed the distraction. She started calling me Toodles after I lost my marbles when I was kid. I didn't understand the nickname until she made me watch *Hook*. I told her I hated the nickname, even though secretly I loved it.

"John! Hello! Earth to John!" Marissa snapped her fingers impatiently at me.

"Jesus! What is your problem?"

Marissa narrowed her eyes at me. "This whole trip was your idea! And now Wonder Scout has gotten us lost—"

"Hey!" Ryan glowered.

Wow, things must really be bad if he's mad, I thought. I shook my head to clear it of the memory of my sister and held up my hand for silence. "Here's what we're going to do. We're going to keep heading down this trail—such as it is—until we find a clearing big enough for all of us to set up camp." I adjusted my pack to take some of the weight off my neck and took the lead.

We walked in silence for several minutes until we had to stop and get our flashlights out. I maintained my silence, trying to focus on keeping the path in my flashlight's beam, not my growing dread.

Marissa and Ryan argued behind me, and three shafts of light wavered around me. Suddenly, off to my right there was a flare of silvery fire that shot above the tree line. "Did you guys see that? That went above the trees!" I asked loudly over the arguing.

"Did we see—" Nova started to ask, but as the flames fell back below the trees, silver embers started to rain down on us like starlight.

"There has to be someone over there. We should go make sure they're okay," I said, concerned.

"John, there is no way I'm going over there. Do you know the kind of magic they could be using?" Ryan asked me through clenched teeth.

"Dude, we have to make sure they're okay! Especially if they're using magic."

"I agree with John, and, besides, I think that we've listened to you long enough," Marissa sniped.

Ryan lowered his head, and I frowned at her. "Ris, I know we're all tired and hungry," I said, trying to be diplomatic, "but something has clearly happened that is out of Ryan's control." I walked closer to Ryan. "Dude, I really don't think we have another choice."

Ryan took a deep breath and turned to Nova, who materialized at his side. "What do you think?"

Nova sighed. "I think that, unless there are a bunch of Unseelies over there, we should take the risk."

Ryan relented, but held on to Nova's hand.

I took my place back at the lead and turned in the direction of the silvery glow. I felt something stir in my memories... No, that wasn't my memory; the vision was trying to push forward. "Dammit! Not now!" I hissed as I shoved the vision to the back of my brain.

Marissa caught up with me. "Hey, are you okay?"

I nodded, my jaw clenched. "Fine. Just really ready to put this pack down."

Marissa squinted at me harshly. "No, I don't buy it. Ever since you got back from your grandma's funeral—"

"Just drop it, okay?" I didn't mean to shout. Marissa's eyes widened, and she fell back toward Ryan as I kicked the ground and felt like a grade A asshole.

"Hello? Is someone there?"

Instinctively, we all turned our flashlights off and stood in stony silence in the growing darkness.

"Please"—it was a woman's voice, and she sounded scared—"if there is someone there, please tell me."

Ryan held a finger to his lips and shook his head. Marissa scowled at him. I shrugged, and Ryan started gesturing wildly.

"H-h-hello?" came another plaintive cry.

We continued our silent argument for a few more minutes before Nova appeared in the middle of our tight circle. Nova looked scared. I wasn't sure where Nova had disappeared to, but they were definitely spooked. Nova held up their hands, and we stopped to pay attention. They pointed to the way from which we had come and raised a hand. Ryan raised his hand too. Nova then put their hand down and pointed toward the fading silvery light. Marissa and I then raised our hands.

Nova moved to stand by Ryan, and for a moment I was afraid that they were going to leave. My final adventure with my best friends, and now we were going to split up.

But no.

Nova held out a fist and tapped it silently three times on their other hand. They looked around at us; reluctantly, we all nodded.

Fists out.

Rock.

Paper.

Scissors.

"*Shoot*," we all mouthed.

I threw rock, and across from me, Ryan had thrown scissors. I dropped my fist onto his hand. Marissa threw scissors, and Nova, paper. Marissa triumphantly cut across Nova's hand.

Marissa and I clinked our flashlights as though they were wineglasses and turned them on. We moved toward the firelight.

*

We broke through the brush and into a clearing. At the very center was a towering column of silver campfire that was slowly receding and fading into yellows and oranges. Behind the flames a woman slowly came into view. She was sitting on a log, her legs crossed in front of her. My gut twisted when I saw her smile. It wasn't right. I blinked, and suddenly her face looked drawn and anxious. There was no sign of a smile—it must have been a trick of the light. I took a step forward, and the woman pulled her shawl tightly around her.

I held up my hands, my flashlight cutting into the night sky. "Whoa. Sorry. We didn't mean to frighten you. We got lost heading for our campsite."

"Dude! We didn't get lost! I could see the rangers' station until the sun went down! And then I could see the lights from it! Just look!" Ryan pointed in the direction we had been heading, and we all turned to look. Where there had been lights in the distance, now there was only darkness. Our landmark was gone.

Marissa slapped Ryan on the shoulder. "My God, Ry! What have we been following all day?"

"I...I don't know."

The young woman pulled a thermos from her small pack and took a drink. "These trails can be treacherous for anyone unfamiliar with them." She smiled down at her thermos as Ryan threw her a dirty look.

I held my arm across Ryan's chest—I could feel him try to start forward. He never got angry, but after the day we had had, it wouldn't take much to set any of us off. I caught Ryan's eye and watched him as he silently begged me to leave with him, to go home.

Nova spoke quietly from the shadows, "Ry, we'll get out of here tomorrow, but we have to rest."

I turned back to the woman. "My name is John. We would really appreciate it if we could share your campsite for the night." The woman didn't answer me right away; she was staring into the trees, her lips pursed with concentration. I followed her gaze; there was nothing there.

She shook her head. "I'm sorry; I thought I heard something. Of course, you can stay here tonight. There is safety in numbers."

I moaned with relief as I dropped my pack from my shoulders. "Thank you."

Marissa dropped to the ground with a huge sigh. Ryan and Nova dropped their packs at the same time, and I saw the woman flinch and squint in Nova's direction.

"You didn't tell us your name," Ryan prompted.

The woman shook her head, her blonde ponytail glittering in the firelight. "I didn't. You're right."

"Will you?" I prodded. She was still looking toward where Nova had been.

"It's Aggie." She turned her face to me and smiled brilliantly.

I smiled back without hesitation. Ryan elbowed me. "What? She's willing to share her camp with us. Relax."

"You don't understand," Ryan whispered vehemently.

"No. You don't understand. You messed up. Own it. It's only one night, and we'll be out of here tomorrow. Maybe Aggie can show us the way back to the trail." I smiled at her again.

"Of course, I will, but you should know that you have wandered really far from any main trail. It'll be quite the hike."

I pulled an envelope of tuna from my pack. "We're up for it."

Aggie leaned back and pulled the oldest guitar I had ever seen out from behind her. Its body was teardrop-shaped, and there was a rose carved around the base. "Do you mind if I play a song? It helps me relax at night, especially after the scare you all gave me."

Marissa answered, "I love music."

"Oh, good. I'm a singer by trade, and in my travels, I've acquired so many stories I've started incorporating them into my songs." From a pouch I hadn't noticed, Aggie grabbed a handful of something and threw it into the fire.

The flames rose, and as the embers floated into the air, they made ripples similar to those caused by rocks skipping on a lake. Then from out of the flames swam a seal. Aggie stared at the flames for a minute and closed her eyes. As soon as she began to sing, I was lost at sea.

1983

Off the coast of Cape Cod, there is an island of rock where pure-white Selkies gather just after the first frost of the year. The residents of the town find the gathering peculiar—seals don't really enjoy lying on cold rocks, yet there they are.

Year after year.

*

Chilled fog slips
Across calm water.
As it clears,
Fishermen see them
Waiting.

*

"You'll watch until I'm gone?" Brin asked her new husband as the boat rocked gently.

Patrick looked bravely at his beautiful bride. "I promised you I would, and I will be waiting right here on the first day of spring." He picked up the fur coat that was as white as the first snowfall, but when Brin tried to take it, Patrick tightened his grasp. "No. Stay with me. I know I promised you and your family that this would be our arrangement, but I have your coat. You have to stay with me." Patrick's eyes grew hard as he continued to refuse to relinquish the fur.

Brin's deep-brown eyes narrowed. "Patrick," she said warningly, "we've been over this. I need to go back. You promised. Give me my coat."

Patrick released the coat with a sigh and lit a cigarette. "I can't believe I let you talk me into this."

Brin smiled and took the cigarette from his lips, crushing it out. "I didn't talk you into anything. You are very lev-elheaded and very understanding." Brin turned her head at the barking from the island. "I'm coming," she called. She looked at Patrick one final time. "Try not to smoke too much while I'm gone."

Patrick looked her up and down and knew he would always remember her this way. Flaming-red hair falling over her shoulder in a thick braid, chocolate-brown eyes shining brightly with unconcealed excitement, and her coat around her shoulders like a cape. She looked like a medieval warrior.

He blinked, and she was gone. In her place was an icy-white seal. She flipped off the boat and swam off.

As promised, Patrick stayed in his rowboat, oars dripping cold seawater onto the deck, and watched Brin swim toward her other family. Then, right before they vanished into the horizon, she turned, leapt out of the water, and waved a flipper at Patrick. "Right," he said, "time to go home."

Patrick slid another cigarette out of his pocket; it was a vice he tried to only allow himself while Brin was gone in the winter. As he relaxed into the rhythmic rowing, Patrick reflected on how his life had turned into a mythic love story.

*

Oars slap the water
Sending ripples out to
Forever.

*

She had been trespassing.

Patrick lived a very solitary life and was angry at having his haven intruded on by this interloper. Patrick was already shouting at her as he tied his pocket trawler to the dock.

She whirled around, wild-eyed. Her skin was as white as the fog that hovered over the top of the sea and kissed the sandy shore in the morning; her hair was blowing in the wind and glowed like the embers of a dying fire. She screamed and grabbed her towel off the beach.

No, not a towel.

A coat.

Before Patrick could reach her, the woman threw her coat over her shoulders and shrank down into the body of a seal. She dove into the foamy waves and vanished.

"What the hell was that thing?"

Patrick spent the next several days researching what he learned were Selkies. It turned out that they were distant cousins of the much more violent Sirens. Selkies, unlike their relatives, lived most of their days as seals, but every so often a human would catch their eye and draw them to land.

"So I caught her eye," Patrick said to himself. He felt smug as he read on and learned that if a human found and successfully hid a Selkie skin, they could keep the Selkie indefinitely. "Keep? Sounds more like kidnapping to me." Patrick felt a little ill and more than a little disgusted at humans' behavior toward magic and its keepers.

Patrick started to keep watch for the Selkie. He wanted was to see her again, to tell her that she would be safe on his beach, to apologize for humanity, and…what? What could he possibly tell her to get her to trust him? *Nothing*, there was nothing. And so, after a few weeks, he gave up hope. *Maybe I wasn't what caught her eye; perhaps it was my private piece of land*, Patrick thought ruefully.

One morning after setting his lobster cages, he motored out to deeper waters to cast his net. He had settled in with a book and a cigarette when he heard a soft bark. He glanced up; there she was, stepping out of her coat on his shore. Patrick yelped as he dropped the cigarette on his lap.

The Selkie straightened, apparently startled by the sound that had carried over the water. He hurriedly brushed the ash off his jeans, pulled his midwater trawlnet back in—after all he had read, he didn't want to risk catching something he hadn't meant to—and headed back to shore.

The Selkie stood unmoving as she watched Patrick come back. He hit the sandy bottom of the shore with a jerk and jumped off the deck of the boat, splashing into the water. Patrick rubbed sweaty hands on his singed jeans and said, "Hi."

She eyed him suspiciously. "Hello."

Patrick stepped forward and was surprised when his foot squelched inside his shoe. "I need to come out of the water.

It's cold. I am not interested in taking your skin. Or keeping you here."

She nodded, but remained on her guard.

Patrick held his hands up and squished the rest of the way to dry land. "My name is Patrick."

"Hello, Patrick."

"Will you tell me your name?"

"No."

Patrick shrugged and pulled a cigarette out of his nearly empty pack. "Okay. Well, I just think that if you're going to trespass on my beach, I should get to know your name."

"That's a gross habit, you know. Gross for everyone. And it smells everywhere, even in the water."

Patrick didn't put his cigarette out. "I will keep that in mind."

The Selkie reached for her skin. "I'm sorry to have trespassed on what you believe is your beach."

*

Out of sight, but
Not out of heart.
The winter nights
Black and long.
Spring not even a
Glow on the horizon.

*

Brin sat hunched over, chewing on what was left of her fingernail and rocking slowly. Patrick stood behind her, wanting so badly to reach out and touch her, to calm the tension in her rigid body, and yet he refrained. From the window, he could see Selkies watching him from the rocky island where they waited every year for Brin; it was his fault that they were still waiting. He should have gone to them sooner to explain the situation. But now…? Well, it was too late.

Brin wouldn't leave the house anymore.

Patrick ran a hand through his curly brown hair and sighed; at the first sign that something was wrong, he should have gone for Brin's family. Every year at the first frost, Brin would bundle into her favorite cardigan—an old wool one that Patrick's mother had knit for him—pull a stocking cap over her cascade of fiery hair, smile brilliantly, and declare, "It's time to say goodbye to the season." The door would slam behind her, and she would walk for an hour or two. Patrick would watch from the kitchen until she disappeared into the trees.

This year had been different. She left and…it was almost ten o'clock at night, and Patrick was still standing at the kitchen window. "What the hell? Brin?!"

Silence answered.

Patrick searched the house, all the while wondering where the day had gone and what happened to Brin. After he ransacked the inside, Patrick ran outside; the small slice of moon barely gave enough light to his dock, let alone the woods surrounding the rest of his land.

A rustling sound to his right made him turn. "Brin! Thank God!"

She tripped forward, a hand pressed to her forehead. "Patrick? Am I home? Thank the goddess."

All concerns about his own missing time flew from his brain as he ran to his wife. "Are you okay? Where have you been?" Patrick cupped her face in his hands, looking for any sign of injury. He pulled a stray dove feather from her hair and watched Brin's eyes go wide.

Brin hugged Patrick to her so tightly he could barely breathe. "I got lost. I am so scared."

That was the start.

When he mentioned a few days later that it was time to get her fur out of the attic, she looked him straight in eyes and said, "What fur? What do you mean?" Patrick had tried to question her further, but she became increasingly agitated, so he left her alone. Brin only remembered her husband and their life together, but nothing that had come before.

At first Patrick was glad her memory was gone. Glad she couldn't remember her family. If Patrick was completely honest with himself, he was tired of sharing her, tired of her leaving every winter to go where he couldn't go. He knew that he should be grateful for how understanding Brin's family were. How terrified they had been as they sat watching from their rock as Brin took human vows and handfasted herself to Patrick. Year after year, Patrick had made good on his promise and let Brin go to her family, but jealousy lurked in the back of his mind. *What does she do with them? Why does she need to go with them every year?*

Now that Brin had lost the memory of who she really was, Patrick rationalized that he wasn't breaking his promise to Brin's family—she was allowed to go see her family anytime she wanted to; she just didn't want to leave anymore. That wasn't his fault. He finally had what he wanted—Brin.

As the seasons changed from fall into winter, Patrick had watched his wife's decline. Now it might be too late to save her. Brin's once-shiny copper hair was lifeless and matted to her head; she had all but stopped eating, and her skin—once luminous with an inner moonglow—was now dull and slightly grey, as though she had not been able to wash all the grime away.

It wasn't just her physical appearance that worried Patrick; it was her growing anxiety. *Anxiety? Ha*, he thought sardonically, *this is paranoia*. Patrick watched Brin jump and jerk every time he moved, and bark at every sound. The sound was inhuman, and it reminded Patrick that Brin's family was waiting outside.

Sighing, Patrick squatted in front of Brin, "Honey, I have to run an errand." He squinted at her. "Do you understand? I will be back in about an hour."

Brin looked through Patrick with wide eyes so dilated Patrick could no longer see the brown of her irises. She continued to chew on her finger. It was bleeding now.

He reached over and pulled her hand from her mouth. Gently, he squeezed her hand. "I'll be back soon."

*

A Selkie longs for
The warmth of human
Love.
And yet
The depths of the sea will
Forever be home.

*

Patrick looked out over the wintry waters and could just make out the soft figures on the rocks in the distance. He stepped onto the swaying rowboat and began the arduous journey of going to see his in-laws. While he rowed, he tried to think of what he would say, how to explain what happened. Sooner than he had hoped, Patrick felt his boat scrape the rocky shore of the small island where Brin's family stood watch. Once he secured his boat, he turned to face them.

The matriarch, Ril, scuttled over, and Patrick kneeled to face his mother-in-law. "Please take off your coat. We need to talk."

Ril tilted her head in understanding and shook off her snow-white skin as though it were nothing more than a hooded jacket. She stood to her full human height and folded the skin over her arm. "Where is my daughter?"

"At home. Safe. Scared, but safe."

"Are you holding her there?"

Patrick knew that he only had honesty going for him here, so he replied, "I was, yes, but now I see. I understand. But something has happened."

Ril put a hand to her mouth. "What have you done?"

Patrick felt the last of his patience snap. "What have I done? What have *I* done? *I* have done everything *you* have ever asked!" He reached into his jacket pocket and pulled out an empty pack of cigarettes, cursed, and crushed it in his fist. "*I* let her come back to you every year, not knowing if you would finally convince her to stay with you or maybe even force her to stay. *I* watch her put that damn skin on every year and dive into the sea and swim off with you, and *I* am alone. All the while wishing she would just stay with me. Be with just me. Well, you know what? I got my wish. She doesn't remember you now. And it's driving her insane."

He had the whole clan's attention now; they started to flank Ril, ready to take out this human interloper without a second thought. Ril raised a hand, and the Selkies relaxed a little. She looked at Patrick and finally seemed to see all of his worry. Ril took a step toward him and asked him to take her to see Brin.

Patrick shrugged. "For all the good it will do." With that, he gestured her on to his boat.

*

Glad to be home and
Free among the rocks and fish
And still longing for
Her Fisherman
At the shore.

*

Brin rushed out of the house and clawed her way into Patrick's arms. "Where did you go? I was alone for so long; you know I don't like to be alone. Why did you leave?"

Patrick wrapped his arms around his wife, at a loss for what to do. "I'm so sorry you were worried. I told you I was leaving, and that I would be back."

Brin was sobbing into Patrick's chest now. "I didn't know. I didn't know. I don't know what's happening. Something is happening. Please tell me what's happening."

Patrick looked helplessly at Ril, who cleared her throat.

Brin looked up with red-rimmed eyes and snot running onto her lips. "Patrick, who is this? Why did you bring this woman here?"

Ril stepped forward. "You really have no memory of me at all? Of your family?"

"Patrick is my family," Brin replied, clutching tighter at her husband.

Ril looked as though she had been slapped. She nodded slightly and walked into the house.

Patrick slowly extracted himself from Brin's grasp and said, "Brin, let's go inside. I won't leave you again. I promise. But we need to hear her out."

"I don't want to talk to her. She scares me." Still, Brin let Patrick lead her inside.

As soon as they were inside, Brin folded herself into her chair by the window, and she stared out.

"Do you want some tea?"

Brin's head snapped back at the sound of her husband's voice. "What?" she asked. "Oh, no, thank you." Brin leaned back in the chair and immediately started rocking.

Ril looked at Patrick, dumbstruck at the change in her daughter. "I'd love some tea, please."

Patrick nodded and put the kettle on the flame. "So, you see, this is what I've been dealing with."

Ril nodded and turned to her daughter. "Brin, please, you must remember something about me. About your life. Anything."

Brin pulled her fingers from her mouth and pursed her lips. "I remember going for a walk, and then I was home" —she looked pointedly at Patrick—"with my family."

"What about before the walk? Your childhood?"

Brin's eyes widened. "Childhood?" She looked at Patrick. "What is she talking about? You said you were my family. My life."

Ril leveled a look at her human son-in-law. "I'm sure he did. And he is...now. But what about before?"

Brin shook her head and started rocking again, repeating, "No...no...no..." to herself before she started humming.

That is new. Patrick turned and looked at Brin. "What is that song?" he asked her.

Brin's humming got louder. It wasn't a tune that he recognized, but Ril had turned sheet-white.

"Show me."

Patrick set the cups of tea down on the table. "Show you what?"

"Show me where she walked."

"Why?"

"Now!"

Patrick looked at Brin as he blew across the lip of his mug. "I don't know where she walks. She told me she goes for these 'frost walks' to say goodbye to the land and get ready for the winter in the waves. She takes the same walk every year, but she never lets me go with her. It's how she gets ready to leave me. Maybe Brin remembers."

Ril ignored her tea and kneeled in front of her daughter; she laid her hands over Brin's and said, "Please. Can you show me where you walked that day?"

Brin lowered her head. "I don't want to. Please don't make go back out there."

"I need to know what happened to you, and I think I can figure it out if you show me."

Patrick watched Brin as she stared down at their joined hands, and when she looked up, Patrick knew that Brin had started to remember.

"I'll take you."

*

> *Though she only proclaims his virtues,*
> *Selkies will never believe that a man,*
> *Any man, will respect their traditions.*

*

Brin barreled into the house, startling Patrick; she wrapped herself around him like a vise. "Please don't make me go again. Please. I'll be fine. But I can't go anymore. I can't leave you ever again. Please."

Patrick scooped her up and, with a terrified look at Ril, carried Brin into their bedroom. He lay with her while she hummed and rocked against his chest. Patrick ran a calloused hand over the knots and tangles in his wife's hair and promised that he wouldn't leave her. "No matter what," he reassured Brin.

Once Brin had fallen into a restless sleep, Patrick rose slowly from the bed and steeled himself to face the wrath of Ril.

"Patrick, we have to get her into the water," Ril stated as soon as he closed the bedroom door behind him.

"No. She's terrified enough as it is; I won't send her somewhere where she is alone."

"She won't be alone; I will be with her."

"She doesn't know what she is!"

"She will learn. You don't get it. She is being eaten alive by that song; this might be her only hope."

"Song? You mean the humming? It's a soothing technique. Kids do it all the time." Even as he said the words, he knew how out of control he sounded.

Ril rubbed the bridge of her nose. "It's a Siren's song."

"A Siren? Here? No, I'm sorry. Brin obviously fell on that walk and hit her head. I can keep her safe here while she heals."

Ril inhaled deeply and thrust a feather at him. "Patrick, we both love Brin, but I need you to hear me. A Siren has taken her memory."

"You expect me to believe that a Siren picked my wife at random, stole her memory, and a *Siren's song* is slowly driving her insane? No, I'm sorry. Sirens kill people. That's why we stay away from that part of the ocean. Only sailors with a death wish go out there."

"Not this Siren. She hasn't been with her sisters for centuries."

"It doesn't matter; what you're saying doesn't matter. Brin stays here…with me. Where she should have stayed all along."

Ril sank onto the sofa and put her head in her hands. Now was not the time for that fight, so she chose a different tactic. "How long have you known that her memory was gone?"

Patrick gripped the back of a chair. "Too long. For that, I'm sorry, but I just wanted her to stay with me. When she's with you, I am always so afraid that she'll decide to stay in the sea. It is her choice, always, but I know that one day she won't choose me anymore."

Ril nodded. "That is the risk in loving us. You are better than most, though; you gave her the choice. You gave her what she needed, always. Yet when it counted, when it really mattered, you kept her away, stole her from us. You were no better than the rest of them."

Kept her. He was doing exactly what the books said he would he do, and he had let Brin down. He *had* kept her. Patrick sat down beside Ril and put a hand on her shoulder. "I'll get her ready. We'll be on the water tomorrow."

Ril looked at Patrick. "Thank you. I don't know if I can help her, but I need to try. She can't live like this anymore."

*

Banished to the sea.

Cursed to live apart.

Two beings. One heart.

*

Patrick placed the folded fur on the bench of the rowboat while Brin stood like stone on the shore. He straightened and looked out to where the Selkies sat waiting. He walked over to where Brin stood rigidly and picked her up. She started to wail and scream at him about how he promised her they wouldn't be apart, how she would never trust him again. It tore his soul apart.

He set her down in the boat, harder than he meant to, and sat facing her. "Listen. This is your last chance. You need this; your family out there needs this. They need you. And you need them too. I'm sorry it has to be this way."

Brin crossed her arms tightly across her body and started humming and rocking. Patrick shoved the boat away from the dock with an oar and began to row. He watched as Brin started to quiet; then she let her arms fall, trailing her fingers through the salty water. She started to remind him of the Brin with whom he had fallen in love. They rode in silence together, and for the first time in over a month, they were both completely relaxed in each other's company.

As they neared the island, Patrick saw Ril slide into the water. He pulled the oars into the boat and picked up Brin's fur. "You need to put this on. It's getting chilly out here."

Brin took the fur and pet it slowly; she raised her eyes to Patrick and nodded. The fur parted easily and slid over her shoulders as though she had never taken it off.

As Ril reached the boat and barked quietly, Patrick reached over and pulled the hood up and over Brin's face. He smiled sadly as she flipped herself off the boat and into the water. For the first time in their marriage, she didn't wave to him before diving under the water.

Ril nodded her thanks and dove under to catch up with her daughter.

*

The buds on the trees,
Misty green.
The air warming while
The sea stays cool.
The Selkies have not appeared.
Still, he waits.

*

That spring, as he always did, Patrick rowed out to the island and waited.

John

I struggled to find my feet under me as the ship rocked in the storm. I squinted through the rain, waiting to get soaked in the deluge, but I remained dry. Waves crashed against the sides of the ship and washed up over the deck. I was blown into the railing and held on for dear life. As I righted myself, I saw two people standing at the front of the ship. One woman was pressed back against the railing, her hair hanging in burnished-gold tangles down her face. The other woman had her back to me and was dressed in all black, so that all I could see was her hair falling out of a bun at the base of her neck.

I started forward to try to hear what they were saying. I couldn't make out the words, but I could tell that they were definitely arguing. The storm obscured what they were saying, and I couldn't even get an idea of what they looked like. To my right, a figure stumbled through a door. He was clutching his head, and instinctually I started forward to help him. He fell through my arms and hit the deck with a thud. Another wave threw me sideways and rolled the man onto his back. I dropped to my knees and crawled forward. I gasped; his face was a mirror of my own. Is this another memory, I wondered.

The rain started to slow down enough so that I could hear the women who were still arguing.

"What do you mean she left you on the island?"

I heard a snarl, and then the other woman answered, "Do you think I would have come looking for you if I weren't desperate?"

The woman with her back to me moved to the side, and I realized the desperate woman was completely naked. What the hell is happening here?

"Honestly? I'm pretty sure you thought I was dead. At the very least, you wanted me dead." She waited a beat then nodded. "Now, I haven't seen our sister since that last day on the island, and I have no desire to ever see either of you again. Fly away."

She turned to face the man on the ground, and I screamed. The woman coming toward us was the same woman who had so graciously welcomed us to her camp. "Hades! How did he get up here? He was supposed to be unconscious."

"So I guess your way *isn't as reliable as the old way, is it?"*

The woman I knew as Aggie looked over her shoulder. "Not when I'm interrupted, no."

I scrambled back as she approached, her dress completely soaked through and dragging behind her. I watched as Aggie's lips peeled back to reveal a row of razor-sharp fangs, and her eyes appeared black.

Suddenly, I couldn't hear the dream anymore; the only sound was the most beautiful singing I had ever heard. I looked around, trying to find where it was coming from, but it seemed to surround me. As the singing reached a crescendo, my vision started to grey —first a softening at the edge, then narrowing with each note.

Suddenly, there was a roaring in my ears as though I had put on earmuffs made of conch shells. The people who remained in my greyed vision didn't seem to hear anything, and I couldn't hear them. The dream seemed to be closing in faster...and then every-thing was gone.

I looked around. "Hello!" I shouted. My voice echoed in the nothingness, and I realized I had never been so alone in my life. I sat down, folded my knees up to my chest, and waited.

*

When I woke up, the sun was above the tree line. My eyes felt gritty, and my back ached.

"Good morning, sleepyhead," Marissa greeted me cheerfully.

I pressed my fingertips against my eyes to rub away the sleep, but wound up taking several eyelashes out too. "Good—ouch!—morning," I grumbled back. "What time is it?"

"Almost ten." I recoiled involuntarily at the voice. "Hey, you okay?" Aggie asked, smiling furtively. "You look terrible."

I forced myself to take a few deep breaths and stretched my legs out in front of me. "Yeah, I'm great. Did I sleep sitting like this?"

Ryan looked over at me concernedly as he strapped his bedroll to the bottom of his pack. "Yes, you did. We tried to lay you down, but your body was so rigid we couldn't move you at all."

"After a few tries, we gave up and settled in to listen to Aggie's music. She is an amazing musician," Marissa said as she wrestled her sleeping bag into something that resembled a roll.

I nodded and absently scratched my ankle. "I'm guessing I missed breakfast."

"Oh yeah, but there's Pop-Tarts and water that we kept out for you."

Out of the corner of my eye, I saw Aggie jump as I caught what Nova tossed me. I ate silently and watched my friends and our host finish breaking camp. I narrowed my eyes at Aggie. "Aren't you going to be hot in that shawl?"

She smiled and shook her head. "No. I'm"—she paused strangely as though she couldn't think of the word—"anemic. I'm cold all of the time."

"You pack really light too. Didn't you say you were a through hiker?"

"John!" Marissa snapped at me.

Nova sat down next to me and hissed in my ear, "Dude, shut up." Their eyes were glued to Aggie.

Aggie smiled a toothy grin at Marissa.

Again I was scared, but I couldn't figure out why.

"It's all right. Yes, I guess you could consider me a through hiker. But, truly, I'm more of a"—she did that thing again, as though she couldn't remember the word—"survivalist. I've lived off of nature and whatever crosses my path for most of my life."

Ryan stood, brushed his hands on his cargo shorts, and said, "Well, I think we should get going. We've imposed long enough."

Aggie arched a brow at Ryan, her smile taking on an edge. "You sure you can find your way today?"

Ryan pointed. "We can see the rangers' station from here. My campsite must be close by."

I nodded and kept scratching my ankle. "Yeah, let's go." The world tilted as I stood and tried to swing my pack onto my back at the same time. I staggered, and Nova grabbed my arm.

"Dude, you have got to keep it together. We need to get out of here," Nova whispered urgently.

"I've got it!" I snapped.

Aggie squinted at me. "None of us said that you didn't. We were just discussing if I should come with you all. At least until you're sure you're at the campsite. I would just be beside myself if something happened that I might have been able to help prevent."

Nova rolled their eyes, and Ryan frowned, but Marissa looked at Aggie with open gratitude and said, "Thank you so much. I would hate to spend another day wandering aimlessly with faulty gear." She shot a look at Ryan, and his frown deepened.

I rubbed my ankle with my shoe and grimaced. "Fine. It's fine. Ryan, you should take the lead."

"But—"

"Marissa, enough. Ryan has been camping here his whole life. I am done blaming him for some random mishap with his compass. Aggie will walk with us because she is right. If we get stranded again, we'll need a survivalist to help get us out of here."

"Fine. I guess I'll just bring up the rear," Marissa replied sounding miffed.

I felt Nova relax slightly. I glanced at them, but they shook their head slowly at me. "Great. Fine. Let's go," I said.

We left the site, Ryan and Aggie in the front, Marissa and I behind.

I stopped. *Where is Nova?* I turned and watched them bend and pick something up from our camp—a giant beige feather. I watched them slip the feather in their pocket before running to catch up with us.

Nova hung behind me as we continued on. "You hanging in there?" they asked.

"Yeah, my head just hurts."

"You do look the worse for wear this morning. What happened to you last night?" They were keeping their voice lowered.

"Why are you whispering?" I demanded, looking over my shoulder at Nova.

Nova glowered at me. "Dammit."

Ryan spoke up suddenly, "Sorry, dude. Aggie and I were just checking the map against what we're seeing around us. If you want to help, you can come up here with us."

Marissa and I exchanged glances. Something was going on, but Marissa and I were being kept in the dark. I knelt down to scratch my ankle; whatever had bitten me must have been huge. "Nope, I'm fine. I just don't like feeling like I'm being kept out of the loop."

Ryan's eyes flicked to Nova. "Sorry. Hey, you know what? Why don't we stop for a break here? Maybe Aggie and I can make sense of why the map doesn't match where we're actually standing."

Marissa dropped her pack gratefully. "Thank God."

I sat down and lifted my pant leg; right above the top of my shoe was an angry-looking scab in a symbol I didn't recognize, but I knew immediately where it had come from.

"Oh my God, John! When did you get a tattoo?" Marissa squealed. She scrambled closer to look. "John, this looks infected. Where did you go? I wish you would have told me; we could have gone to my guy."

I rolled my eyes. "I went to my nan's…artist. It was a sort of dedication to her."

"Ryan, we have to get to that rangers' station. This needs to be looked at," Marissa said while opening her first aid kit and handing me some antibiotic ointment.

"Absolutely. Sorry, John, but it looks like we need to cut this trip short."

I hung my head. "Guys, this is all my fault. I'm sorry I pushed this trip on all of you. I just wanted one more big story before"—I hesitated; they could never know—"graduation."

My friends all nodded at me, but Aggie, who was perched on a rock, was mindless, strumming her guitar. Quietly, she started humming along.

I felt my eyes grow heavy. I was so tired. Maybe I would just rest my eyes until it was time to start moving again.

800 BCE

Sun over the horizon.
I bask.
I breathe in its rhythm to forget.
humming

*

Something had entered her waters. Amphitrite tilted her head back and watched as all the schools of fish suddenly froze and just hovered in the water, as though someone had paused all living things. Even the solitary shark had abandoned its stealthy glide to stare, without seeing, into the depths of the ocean. Amphitrite narrowed her eyes; whatever it was did not belong here. "Time to go see what we've caught." Taking up her black mother-of-pearl scepter, Amphitrite pushed off toward the surface.

She could taste the blood before she saw it. The salty water began to burn her gills with iron. Amphitrite paused in her ascent and looked toward the surface. Through the clear water, there was a trail of rust that led up to a figure floating on the surface. "There you are." Amphitrite continued slowly rising to the surface; after several feet, a feather floated down in front of her face. She plucked the feather out of the current and chewed the inside of her cheek. *No,* she thought, *it can't be.*

Still studying the feather, Amphitrite let the salty water push her to the surface. Fish continued to remain paralyzed in the water; they got stuck in Amphitrite's twilight-blue tentacles, while seahorses got tangled in her kelpy tresses. Amphitrite shook all the sea life free and tried to send them on their way so they wouldn't get caught in a wayward fisherman's net.

When she broke the surface of the water, Amphitrite kept her distance from the floating figure. She kept only her eyes above the water and her body still so as not to alert her prey. Slowly, the current guided the sea goddess around so that she could see with whom she was dealing.

Well, well, she thought, grinning broadly, *it seems that this humble servant has forgotten her place.* Amphitrite swirled her tentacles to push her farther out of the water, and then she waited to be acknowledged. She was, after all, married to one of the most powerful gods; she deserved to be treated with respect.

Impatiently, Amphitrite inspected her cuticles, one tentacle gently slapping the surface of the water. "Zeus be damned. Uh, *hello.*"

The intruder jerked in the water. "My goddess!" Sea-glass eyes met hurricane-grey ones. "Amphitrite, my lady."

Amphitrite held up a hand dismissively. "Took you long enough. You are outside of the boundary. But you knew that."

Aglaope carefully treaded water and maintained wary eye contact with the queen of the sea. "Yes, I know. But I had no choice."

Amphitrite touched the head of her staff to the water and glided gently forward.

Aglaope instinctively backed away.

"What happened to you?"

Aglaope sighed. "Sibling squabbles."

"A squabble that left you bleeding in the sea, asking for certain death? Zeus, I'm glad they're not my sisters."

"Yeah"—Aglaope choked out a short laugh—"me too. Listen, please, I won't bother anybody. I just need to get to land."

Amphitrite threw her head back and laughed. "Won't bother anybody? You have already bothered me. Your singing has all but stopped the sea life from existing. I can't even imagine how Poseidon will react when he returns. And what about poor Demeter, whom you betrayed so completely." Amphitrite's smile turned into a sneer. "She's been waiting for a reason to meet with you again."

Aglaope's sun-bronzed skin turned stark white. "Well, she couldn't do much more to me." She turned in the water so that Amphitrite could see the source of the bleeding.

Amphitrite gasped. "You…you're…mutilated! What happened?"

Aglaope lay back in the water, ignoring the bite from the salt water in her wounds. "We had a difference of opinion, and I was outvoted."

A wave rose under Amphitrite, pushing her farther out of the water. "You will tell me the truth or—"

"Or what?" Aglaope trilled her fingers through the water. "What could you possibly do to me?"

Swirling her staff in the water, Amphitrite rode a foamy wave over to where Aglaope floated. She wrapped her tentacles around Aglaope's arms and yanked Aglaope from her repose. Amphitrite pressed the inky, pearlescent spikes of her scepter under Aglaope's chin. "What could I do? I could—"

Aglaope swallowed hard. "My sisters have turned on me. And rightly so, I guess. I have been betrayed and exiled. Death would be welcome."

Amphitrite's stormy eyes narrowed; the foaming waves keeping Amphitrite and Aglaope aloft softened. "You say you have been betrayed, and yet you will not offer up the offenders. Why?"

"Because their betrayal is my true punishment. They are free of me, and I am lost to them."

"And still you braved the sea, knowing the punishment that awaited you." Amphitrite wondered what hand Fate had in this chance meeting, and why it had been she, not Poseidon, who had noticed the change in the water. "Are you sure the betrayal was so complete that you would not be welcomed back?"

"Milady, they took my wings. I no longer have sisters. And nowhere to go. With all due respect, I don't see how it could be any less complete."

"And yet"—Amphitrite dropped her staff and let Aglaope fall back into the water—"the sea is unusually calm today. It would be a shame if the weather were to turn suddenly."

Aglaope grimaced. "So you're going to let the sea take care of me, then, instead of killing me yourself."

Amphitrite rubbed her temples. "Hear me, child. The Fates, or someone, have sent you to me instead of to Poseidon. Your life is in my hands. And even though the news of you and your sisters' plot—and eventual failure of said plot—did reach me here in the depths I find that I feel…empathetic to your current plight. So, I say again, it would be a shame if the weather were to turn and you slipped through my fingers."

Aglaope's face turned hopeful as she bobbed in the water, but then she frowned. "And what would I owe you in return?"

"That is the question, isn't it?" Amphitrite slowly rotated her staff in her fingers; the fish that were suspended between its two tines glistened in the sun. "Really, I suppose it will depend on what I learn from your sisters. You might not owe me anything, but if I discover that this has all been a ruse and you played on my sympathies, I will find you. And your punishment will not be swift." Amphitrite leaned down and pulled feathers from Aglaope's arm. "I'll need these. Proof, you understand."

Aglaope nodded, but found she didn't actually understand.

"Now, go." Amphitrite raised her staff, and a strong wind blew the queen's hair back from her face as the sky darkened.

Aglaope was lifted in the stormy seas and whisked off for lands unknown.

*

Ribs expand.
Pain sears.
My physical reminder of the cost.
humming

*

Amphitrite watched Aglaope be taken off and said a small prayer for her. Once Aglaope was out of sight, Amphitrite sighed heavily; she loved the sea, but the arrangement with her husband often left her out of the important dealings.

When Hades was able to steal Persephone because of the Siren sisters' lackadaisical guarding of her, Poseidon had ridden a hurricane to Olympus to weigh in on the punishment, leaving Amphitrite to wonder at the details of what actually happened. Poseidon had been gone for days, and when he returned, he brought the storm with him.

"Those…those…women! They dared to remain silent when faced with us! Well, they have their just desserts now! Let's see if they get any meals anytime soon! Ugh! I told Demeter that she never should have trusted them! But no! Because who better to protect her beloved daughter than" —he sneered—"man-eaters. Well, obviously she was wrong."

Amphitrite had sat quietly while her husband continued to storm around. There was nothing to say when he was in these moods. Poseidon finally stopped in front of his wife and fell to his knees. She wrapped him in her tentacles and placed her hands on either side of his face.

"You've had a rough few days. I wish I could have been there to help."

Poseidon yanked his face away, his barnacled beard scraping her hands. "Do you think I would ever let you up there? With *them*? All their politics and collusion! No, I have to keep you safe, here with me."

Amphitrite looked down at her hands. She knew that Poseidon believed he was protecting her, but she also knew that if she were allowed up there, her darling husband would have to explain his own collusion to her. She sighed, and little bubbles escaped her gills. "Of course, how silly of me."

As time passed, Amphitrite got bits and pieces of what happened from lesser water goddesses and sea nymphs. And, because it was her duty, she had sided with her husband and their family.

Now, though, as she tightly clutched the bloody feathers in her fist, Amphitrite wondered at her defiance. What had made her go to the surface? What would she tell Poseidon? "Nothing. He needs only know what his siblings tell him."

With a flick of her staff, the grey sky turned sickly green. Wind and waves kicked up, and Amphitrite turned her face into the pelting rain. She sank back down into the water, and her tentacles pushed her through the storm toward Siren Rock.

*

The water carries me to
The unknown and still
I pray for death.

*

Amphitrite landed hard on the rocky shore and looked around. Even in the rain, she could tell that this was a prison.

"Sirens!" she shouted into the rain. There was no answer. "Blast this storm!" she yelled, conveniently forgetting that she had created it in the first place. She stabbed her scepter into the rocks, and light speared out of the pearl at its center. "Sirens! Come forth!"

From a cave emerged two women, identical to the one Amphitrite had just sent into the storm. The only telling differences were their wings and the blood on their hands. "Why have you come here?" the one with raven wings asked.

Amphitrite's seaweed brow rose. "My, aren't we impudent."

The other spoke up, "I'm sorry, my lady. My sister forgets herself." Peisinoe elbowed her sister. "What brings you, Queen of the Sea, to our humble island?"

Amphitrite held out a fistful of wet feathers. "I have some questions."

JOHN

Well, this is weird, *I thought as I stood looking down at myself. I remembered this day. It was only a few days after...* "Nan's death," *I whispered to myself. I was so desperate to get away, to escape what was now my sealed fate, that I'd sent a message using Group Chat.*

John: Let's go camping.

Ris: But it's almost finals.

John: Exactly. I need a break. I gotta get out of here.

Ry: I know a place.

Ris: I have too much studying to do. I think I'll skip this one.

Nova: I don't think camping is a good idea. The headlines have been full of campers vanishing. It's creepy. Why don't we just blow off some steam at a bar?

John: Come Ris! We're graduating in two weeks, and I'm all twitchy. Let's just get out of here.

Ry: I'm in.

John: Excellent!

Ry: But you guys are going to have to follow my lead. Nova's right. There have been a lot of people going missing, and I know the trails we'll be taking. I'll keep us safe.

John: Nova's with you?

Nova: No. I'm texting. On the group chat. Right here.

Ris: Sorry about that. I didn't see your text either. What missing campers?

Nova: *sigh* Don't any of you read the news?

Ry: It'll be okay, Nova. We'll only be gone a few days. And my campsite is the one I've been going to almost my whole life. It's not like we're thru-hikers or anything. It'll be great.

Ris: Thru what now?

Ry: Never mind. Nova and I are in.

John: YES! Come on Ris! You know you want to.

Ris: Fine. But I'm bringing my books.

I watched myself lay the phone on his chest as he closed his eyes. "Don't go," I said to myself. "Something terrible is happening."

I heard the singing again, and my apartment whirled around me. Then I was standing in front of my first English class of college. Four years before.

"Hindsight is twenty-twenty," I muttered as I could plainly see whom I had missed those years ago. I had been looking for a seat, and thought I had found one next to a guy with shaggy black hair hanging in his face. "There's some—!" I started to call out, but stopped short. These were just memories; no one could hear me.

"Hey!" a voice shouted. I watched my former self stand and suddenly see—finally!—Nova.

"You look like you belong in a Manga."

Ryan laughed while I cringed at my past self; I didn't give an apology, didn't acknowledge how I almost sat on another person. I just startlingly looked at Nova's silver hair and eyes. I was a real winner.

The singing became louder, and the room whirled again.

"Where am I now?" I turned around and saw, to my surprise, that I was in my apartment, but this time it was empty. Well, mostly empty. There were plastic crates and empty take-out containers. I didn't even have a garbage can yet.

I smiled at this memory.

There was a knock at the door, and I waited for my past self to open it. Nova stood at the door; they were the last person I thought would show up. I liked Nova, but often forgot they were there. Ryan seemed to be the only one who could see Nova all the time.

More loud singing, the memory tornadoed, and I was standing in a bar.

"Oh God. Not this one. God, this is like A Christmas Carol. I have zero desire to stay here." I strode through the crowd, looking for my friends. I found them at a high-top table, waiting for our first All Twenty-One shots and Nova's return from their travels. Ryan had been quiet all night, and I remembered thinking that Nova was different too. More in control of themselves, but also edgier. The silver in their hair and eyes was more of a gunmetal now, instead of the starlight I could only sort of remember.

We were laughing and had just thrown back our first shots when a beast of a man fell into Ryan. The man was apologizing to Ryan when Nova stepped up and got in his face. I watched as Marissa and I stood staring at the scene unravel. Ryan tried to diffuse the situation, but the man was angry at Nova and flicked Ryan away *like a bug. Finally, my past self seemed to wake up, and I tried to insert myself into…what? What was I going to do?*

I laughed because, looking back, I knew I was lucky that I didn't get killed that night. I took one punch, and I was on the ground. Not unconscious, but down. Nova knelt down to check on me and then stood to grab the man by his shirt. Nova's eyes glowed, and they whispered something in the dude's ear. The color drained from his face, and he took off.

The singing got louder again, but this time everything faded to nothing grey.

*

My eyes opened; Aggie was gripping my hoodie and shaking me. "I'm up. I'm awake. Jesus!"

Marissa put a hand to my forehead. "Dude, what is going on with you?"

I shook my head to clear it. "Nothing. I'm fine."

Ryan knelt down in between Aggie and Marissa. "No, you are not." He looked at Aggie. "Excuse me," he said coldly.

She put her hands up in surrender and moved away.

"Dude, what happened? I closed my eyes for a second while you and Aggie tried to make sense of the map, and then she was shaking me!"

"You passed out. We couldn't wake you. It really scared us."

"Yeah, and I think your infection is getting worse," Marissa added, gesturing at my forearm, where another symbol had scabbed over; red veins were snaking out from it. "How many tattoos did you get, man?"

"Too many." I tried to stand up, but bumped into something that had me sitting back down. Ryan and Aggie looked in the direction of what I had hit, but I couldn't see anything there.

Marissa put her hand on my arm. "I think John should stay here while we go on to the rangers' station."

"No, I'm fine. Help me up. Let's just get out of here."

Marissa grabbed me by my arm and pulled me up with the force of two people.

"WOW! Have you been working out? That was amazing!"

Marissa gave me the weirdest look and then looked at my other side. "Are you sure you should be coming with us? You seem really out of it."

I jerked my arm out of Marissa's grasp and started scratching it. "I'm out of here." I stomped off in the direction of the rangers' station. My head was pounding, my tattoos were hot and itchy, and I couldn't focus. We had to get out of there.

Aggie caught up with me and said, "I really do think we should stop. Your friends can keep going. I have ribbon; they can mark branches as they go so that they can find their way back to us with help."

"Dammit! I said I'm fine!" I went down. Flat out. Stars filled my vision. "Okay, go get help," I muttered, spitting out dirt and leaves.

Ryan and Marissa looked at each other and then looked away, whispering. Probably trying to hide their laughter. Aggie stepped over me and set her pack down. I watched her pull a handful of orange ribbons out of her too-small pack and hand them to Ryan. She gestured as she spoke quietly with my friends.

I pushed myself to my knees and started to brush myself off. Aggie sat down next to me and started strumming her weird-shaped guitar. I grabbed the neck and pulled the guitar out of her hands. "No offense, but my head is killing me. I just need silence."

"No offense taken. This must be difficult. It being your last hurrah and all."

"You have no idea." Leaves rustled and crunched on the other side of me. I could have sworn I felt a finger rest on my lips. I rubbed my mouth.

"I think I do. You and I are very similar, you know. Both StoryKeepers…in a way."

My eyes flew open. "How did you know?"

Aggie's eyes shuttered for a moment before she smiled. "I suspected when I saw the rune on your ankle. It's a shame that it seems the ink was contaminated."

"You have them too?"

"No, I keep my stories in my music. You've been so weighed down with the knowledge of your family, that you haven't been able to really hear any of my stories."

"I know. I'm sorry. Your music is beautiful, but my head. I can't stand the pain."

"It's okay. You just rest." Aggie patted my hand, and fleetingly I noticed that her nails were black and curved like a witch's.

The thought was gone as quickly as it came because as soon as my eyes shut, memories started floating by in my mind. Some of them I recognized, most I didn't. I could feel my heart beat in time with each memory. Then the images started to follow another beat. A song. A wordless song that made each of my memories glow before they faded away. I could feel each of the tattoos warm on my skin until all that was left burning was my heart rune.

My sister, Zelda, stood before me. She looked so sad. I could feel my chest burning, but I couldn't wake up. She cupped my cheek in her hand, and I saw tears fall as she turned and walked into the ether.

1750

> *Left. Right. Tighten.*

Creak.

> *Left. Right. Tighten.*

Creak.

> *Left. Right. Tighten.*

Creak.

The woman in the chair stopped rocking, and her dull eyes drifted over the dusty loom sitting under the cloudy window. The song got louder. It always got louder when she looked at it. Louder still when she reached out to stroke the wood. She sighed. It became an unbearable screeching when she tried to remember how to use it.

> *Left. Right. Tighten.*

Creak.

> *Left. Right. Tighten.*

Creak.

> *Left. Right. Tighten.*

Creak.

Some days, she had enough determination to fight through the never-ending music and sit at the loom. Once, she even had the strength of will to take wool down and try to string the loom. She screamed in pain as she forced her hands through motions that once had come so naturally to her. People on the street stopped to stare at her through the window she never bothered to clean anymore. She didn't care. Her life had been taken from her. And for what? She strained to remember, but all she could hear was that damn song.

Finally, she dropped the fiber and fell to the floor, sobbing. She raked her nails down her face, leaving red trails in the hollows of her cheeks. She pounded her fists on the floor, screaming. Who could leave a person this way, rip away her life's passion and leave only a song? A song that never stopped; it was all-consuming. Eating, dressing, working —nothing mattered. She had to consciously remind herself, through all of the noise, to do each of those things...and even sometimes to breathe.

Even now, just thinking about the pain she put herself through to do something she remembered loving, the song grew louder in her head and blocked everything out. She started rocking again.

> *Left. Right. Tighten.*

Creak.

> *Left. Right. Tighten.*

Creak.

> *Left. Right. Tighten.*

Creak.

Rocking in time with the music that no one else could hear, the woman gripped the armrests of her chair until her knuckles turned bone-white. She glared out of the window into the town square. That's where *she* set up. That's where *she* ruined everything.

*

Market Day. Constance smiled as she opened her door and positioned the rock to hold it ajar. It was her favorite day, especially in the late spring, before it became too hot to do anything but sit and hope for sales, and after the crushing business of the winter, when everyone in town wanted new cloaks and shawls. The late spring was when she was able to weave mostly for herself and allowed herself time to chat with townspeople who came in to visit and bring her news of her neighbors.

She sat at her loom and smiled at the fabric she was creating—a rug for her hearth. Decorative rugs were a luxury; they were usually made from fabric that was one step away from the rag pile. Strips of the worn material were braided and then stitched together with a thick needle and sturdy wool thread; she sold all the supplies needed to make one of those types of rugs.

Instead of rags, this one was woven together from pieces of old dresses that she could no longer wear. Every row of every color held a special place in her memory. The strips of fabric were mostly made of wool, but there were a few that were cotton. She didn't think that the cotton strips would hold up very long, but she loved the different textures that they created. With each over-under motion back and forth, she could imagine how the firelight would illuminate the colors. She smiled to herself.

"Wool gathering, Miss Constance?"

Constance blinked and smiled into the face of her most favorite customer. "It would seem that way, Mrs. Howell."

Sarah Howell was smartly dressed in a white blouse, with a blue skirt that covered her tattered, black, lace-up boots. She wore a shawl that matched the skirt; it was held in place by a pin that had an opulent, pearl-accented fleur-de-lis at its top. It was an extravagance that Constance knew Sarah had inherited from her mother, an antique with which she would never part, no matter how dire her family's situation became.

Sarah was Constance's favorite customer not because she regularly purchased from Constance. Quite the contrary, in fact. It was Constance who purchased wool from Sarah's husband. It was the roughest wool of the surrounding farms, but still she bought as much as she could afford. It was this wool that she spun into the heavy-duty rug yarn. That was all it was good for. No, Sarah was Constance's favorite because of the friendship that they had cultivated over the handful of years they had known each other.

The core of their friendship was the news Sarah always brought with her. Babies who were born, mothers who needed a little extra love because their babies didn't make it, what new musicians and players would be visiting—Sarah knew it all. None of it was idle gossip. Sarah did not spread malicious rumors; she only came in with news that she had gotten from the source. It was a rare quality, to Constance's mind, and one that made her day all the brighter when Sarah sat and watched Constance work.

Sarah sat down in the rocking chair opposite the loom and arranged her skirts carefully over her ankles. "Did you hear? There's a musician coming."

Constance looked up. "I did hear that. He's supposed to be a fan of the drink, from what I understand."

Sarah leaned in. "No"—her eyes widened with the scandal she was about to impart—"he was found murdered on the side of the road. The woman who found him was another traveling musician, and she's the one who's coming here."

Constance's hands stopped working, and she looked at her friend closely. "Are you sure? Things have been pretty quiet around here; maybe this is just a rumor."

Sarah shook her head so vehemently her hat wobbled. "Miss Constance, all of this is true! My husband heard it from the doctor who came to help our ewe along with the lambing. You know his home is way outside of town. Dr. Smith said he heard from the horse's mouth, so to speak." Sarah smiled at her pun.

"Meaning what, exactly?"

"Meaning, he had to calm the woman who found the minstrel's body. She was in a terrible state; she came running down the street, tripping over her own feet, and basically fell at the good doctor's door!"

Constance sharply inhaled and sat back in her chair. "No!"

Sarah held a hand up. "Hand to God, Miss Constance. Anyway, the veterinarian said that after a day or two's rest, she should be right as rain and able to play for us right in the town square."

"Well, I'm glad that she'll be okay." Constance had her head back in her weaving.

Sarah sat with her for another few minutes before standing and straightening her skirt. She said, "Well, I have more shopping to do, and you know William; he just hates when I dally too long here."

Constance smiled. That man didn't hate a thing that Sarah did, but she understood that there was actual shopping that needed to be finished. "Of course. You stop by again soon, and please tell your husband that I'll be in need of another bag of wool soon. I'm hoping to get some more of the grey."

Relief brightened Sarah's smile. "I will do that. Thank you."

*

By the time the next Market Day rolled around, the whole town was bustling with news of this mysterious musician who had literally fallen into town. Constance sat in her rocking chair, carding wool that Sarah's husband had brought by earlier that week. It had been an interesting week, hearing people talk about the newcomer, mainly because everyone Constance spoke with had been so vague.

Evidently, the newcomer was blonde and tall for a woman, but the main focus of everyone with whom Constance had spoken was that this woman's voice was like an angel's. Other than that, though, no one could tell Constance anything. They couldn't even tell Constance the musician's name, which she thought was odd, but the people in town brushed her off, telling her that she was worried for no reason.

She was told at every turn what a great guest this traveling musician was and how she only stayed with each family one or two nights because she didn't want to impose. "And," one woman told Constance when she was picking up the new winter cloak Constance had made for her, "she paid for her stay with us with a song she wrote just for us. It was so beautiful and relaxing. I've never slept as well as I did that night."

That seemed absurd to Constance. Goods were dear in this town, and most people were usually willing to barter for something they needed. Who needed a song?

Constance was so focused on her work that she didn't realize she had a visitor until a shadow fell across her loom. She smiled when she looked up at Sarah. "Good morning, Mrs. Howell. How long have you been standing there?"

Sarah continued to only stand over Constance.

Constance stood and looked at Sarah more carefully. Her coat was misbuttoned, and her hair, which was usually carefully pinned into place, fell in mousy-brown snarls around her shoulders. Her shawl hung off one arm and dragged behind her on the dusty ground; the shawl pin was missing.

"Sarah? What's happened? Is it your husband? Has there been an accident?" Sarah did not acknowledge that Constance had spoken, so Constance shook Sarah and started to shout her name.

Finally, Sarah seemed to come out of her daze; she look around confusedly. "Miss Constance? What am I doing here? What happened?"

"What do you mean?"

"Well, last night it was our turn to host the traveling player at our home, and I must have fallen asleep. Now I'm here."

Constance stood back, staring agog at Sarah. "Do you remember anything about last night?"

Sarah shook her head. "I need to sit down. I feel light-headed."

"Of course, please sit here."

Sarah lowered herself into the rocking chair and leaned back.

Constance carefully sat back down at the loom, but didn't resume working. She let Sarah rock slowly for a few minutes before asking, "So you let that woman stay at your house?"

Sarah opened her eyes and raised her head slightly. "Well, of course. It was the neighborly thing to do. After she found that body on the side of the road, she needs all the help she can get."

Constance narrowed her eyes. "She's been here over a week now though. Why hasn't she started her town performances?"

Sarah shrugged. "She's getting there; just give her time. But don't worry. You'll hear her soon. And you'll love her voice as much as I do."

"What's she like?"

"Well, she's blonde, very tall, extremely respectful, and has a voice like an angel."

Constance rolled her eyes. "That's what everyone says. You are always able to get people to tell you everything. She didn't give you a name or anything?"

"A name?"

"Her name. She didn't tell you her name?" Constance was getting impatient. Sarah was never this dull. There was something very wrong.

Sarah yanked her fingers through her tangled hair. "Oh, Miss Constance, I don't know. We talked late into the night, and then she insisted on singing for us. Then I was here. Who can remember all the details of our conversations?" Sarah stood suddenly and said, "I'm sorry. I need to go home. Please, everything is fine."

Constance took the shawl from Sarah, shook it out, and knotted it securely around her friend's shoulders. "Sarah, where is your pin?"

Sarah looked at Constance quizzically. "What pin?"

"Your gold-and-pearl shawl pin. You always wear it."

Sarah yanked her arm away with more anger than was warranted. "Miss Constance, I believe you have me confused with one of your many other patrons. I have never had something that audacious, gold or otherwise. You know we don't have that kind of money, and I feel very upset you would make light of it."

*

By the following week, Constance had just about driven herself out of her mind, trying to find out more about this musician. She hadn't learned anything new about the musician directly, but because of her encounter with Sarah and the missing pin, she started to take note of other missing things. *No,* Constance thought, *not just things. Skills, memories. All gone.* Not only had the people in town forgotten these details, but also they had gone on living their lives as though nothing were lost.

Taken, Constance corrected herself, *not forgotten.* A person can't forget how to sheer a sheep, or how to tell when their tomatoes are ready to pick. Yet there it was—people had lost their livelihoods because they suddenly believed they'd never performed those tasks before.

Constance sat down at her loom and set her mug of steaming tea on the window ledge. She had just started the rhythmic movements of moving the weft right and left across the warp of the loom when she felt it. Lifting her head and brushing strands of hair out of her face, she sat back.

Music, I'm feeling music. How does a person feel music? Constance turned her head and looked out the window to the town square, where she could see that a crowd had gathered. There in the center was the mysterious musician. She was standing on the raised-stone edge of the fountain in the center of the square. Constance was taken aback. Even if she hadn't been balanced on the ledge, the musician still would have towered over the crowd. Constance struggled to see more, but her store was set back from the square, and she couldn't take in the scene the way she wanted to.

Eventually, Constance tried to go back to her weaving. This was insanity; there had been traveling performers of all kinds during her time of living here in town, and she had never before heard them from her store. She furrowed her brow and looked closely at her work. "Dammit." Constance threw the weft down on the fabric stretched in front of her. Back several rows, she had made an error, and now she would have to tear it all back out.

She stood from the loom, hands on her hips; she couldn't concentrate because of the music. Walking slowly to the door, she watched as a few people had started to drift away from the town square; they appeared to be in the same foggy state as Sarah had been the week prior, but they had vague smiles on their faces, and they were all saying the same word. No, not a word. A name. "Agatha."

Constance rubbed her arms as a sudden chill ran over her. She continued to move forward, conscious of every step she took. When she reached the edge of the town square, she locked eyes with the woman commanding her audience and found herself fighting back blackness. Constance stopped, thinking she was about to faint. She turned and went back to her shop, and for the first time since she first opened her shop, she closed early.

*

Constance worked behind closed doors for the next several days; her movements felt sluggish and painful. Twice, she threaded her loom incorrectly, and more times than that she had to tear out entire projects. Things as simple as place-mats came off the warp a knotted mess, and, still, Constance forced herself to work. This is how she made her living. If she couldn't finish these orders, she would starve. She was cursing herself over a shawl when the door opened.

"I'm not open to customers today. Sorry," Constance said, not even looking up.

"I'm not a customer. I'm here to learn."

Constance looked up and clenched her fists. "Haven't you *learned* enough?"

"Not yet. You left before I could finish my song." The woman gave Constance a tight-lipped smile. "Are you having problems with your hands?"

Constance unclenched her hands and forced them to relax. "No, I'm fine. Now, if you'll excuse me, I need to concentrate."

"But I've written a song for you. I've been watching you since I arrived in the square, you know. You ignored me when I was calling for you. I want to know how you did it, and I would love to finish learning how to weave and"—the musician twisted her face into an expression that resembled thinking—"knit. That's it. That's the other skill that's in there."

"Calling me? What are you talking about?"

The woman waved a slender hand dismissively. "Called you. Sang to you. Whichever. I know you heard me. You almost came to the square. What stopped you?"

Constance stood and crossed her arms. Though the woman in her shop still loomed over her, Constance felt more on an even footing with her. "You stopped me. I could see your eyes from the edge of the crowd, and I saw them turn to stone. Whatever you are, whatever you are doing, you are hurting these people. My people. You won't get me."

The other woman nodded and shrugged. "All right. Obviously, you're just too strong for me. Before I go, though, might I sit and watch you finish your work?"

"I'd rather you didn't."

"I'll just take my leave, then."

Constance watched as the woman picked up her lute, glided outside, and headed toward the town square. Constance firmly shut the door and locked it before she bent back over the shawl and began to work.

Unbidden, the words of the song drifted into Constance's shop. The tune was catchy, and Constance found herself moving the weft in time with the song. Constance squinted. *No, she isn't going to win. This is my life, and I am going to keep it.*

The song grew louder, and Constance looked out the window; there in the town square was the musician, strumming her lute and aiming her piercing gaze right at Constance's shop. How was it possible that Constance could hear the song so clearly? *It's not possible.* She shook her head and leaned over the loom. Before she finished an inch, the weft clattered to the floor, and Constance gritted her teeth at the song that was playing over and over in her head. It got louder the more Constance tried to work through it.

Left. Right. Tighten.
Left. Right. Tighten.
The Weaver wefts across her warp.
Images of sea and fields of green
She brings to life with yarn.
She works as Fate,
Controlling the yarns of life.
Left. Right. Tighten.
Left. Right. Tighten.

In the days that followed, Constance continued to try to fight through the music; people stopped coming into her shop, and often avoided her side of the street altogether because of the shouts of frustration and crashing of shelves. When she could take no more, Constance threw her head back, let out one short scream, and let the darkness take her.

*

Hours later, the townspeople heard the shrieks and came running to the weaver's shop. It took three men to restrain Constance. When they finally got her still, the doctor was able to sedate her and examine her injuries. All her injuries were self-inflicted—long scratches down her face and splinters of wood in her hands from the chair that was smashed to pieces. The people in the town couldn't fathom what happened, but whispers started that it was because she was unmarried.

"Unmarried women of a certain age just lose control of their faculties," Sarah told her husband while shaking her head sadly. "I saw it coming the last time I visited her; she asked me, quite cruelly, about a shawl pin that we never could have afforded."

Everyone was so distracted by Constance's breakdown that no one noticed the musician, wrapped in a fine wool cloak, which was secured with a fleur-de-lis pin, leave town without a backward glance.

JOHN

I woke up. In the dark. Alone. Panic set in immediately. Why am I out here alone? I looked around for a backpack, a cell phone, anything. *I came out to the woods with nothing?*

A twig snapped behind me. "Hello?"

"Come on!" a distant voice called.

"Who's there?"

"We have to go right now!" The voice sounded both very close and far away at the same time. Almost like an echo.

There was something pulling my arm; I struggled back against it. "No! I can't see you. I can't see anything. I need to stay put until morning."

"John! We have to go! We need to run! She's coming back!"

"John. Who's John?"

"Dammit! That's you!"

"No, my name is… Oh my God! Why can't I remember my name? What's happening to me?"

Something grabbed my shirt and yanked me forward. *"I need you to open your eyes. It's me!"* The voice was coming from everywhere.

"My eyes *are* open!" I pulled myself free of whatever had ahold of me and spun around. In front of me was a beautiful woman. "Thank God! A person! Please help me!"

The woman tilted her head, and tangled hair fell across her face. "So"—in the moonlight, I could see a thin smile spread across her teeth—"she's left me another one."

"Another what?" I took a step back. This woman's voice did not sound as if it were the one I had been hearing.

"You'll see." I heard a scream from below me as I was yanked into the air.

The Velvet Darkness

An Interlude

N ova ran blindly through the night. Their only thought was to get back to their friends. The moon was finally climbing into the sky, so they could see the trail in front of them. Nova stopped to orient themselves; hands braced on their knees, Nova breathed in deeply through their nose and out their mouth.

Nova looked back down the trail in the direction that Aggie had pointed Ryan. Ryan was an experienced enough camper and hiker that Nova *knew* without a doubt that he absolutely had hung the ribbons that Aggie gave him. But Nova was also just as sure that Aggie had pulled the ribbons down as she made her way toward them, leaving John alone. *John.* Their breath shuddered.

Nova straightened and made their way down the trail, hoping that if they stayed the course, eventually they would find their friends. It was too dark to see the path clearly, so Nova slid their phone from their pocket and turned on the flashlight. They shone a beam of light on the ground at their feet and continued to make their way slowly down the miniscule trail.

After what felt like an eternity to Nova, they stopped again and waved the flashlight around in a tight circle. As Nova came back around, something caught the edge of the light. Focusing their phone on the object, Nova smiled tightly. "Gotcha," they said, walking to the edge of the trees.

Nova bent at the waist, picked up the dusk-colored feather, slid it into their pocket, and then, a few feet away, saw another feather stuck in the bushes. Grimly, they followed the accidental trail.

*

Nova quietly slid into their friends' camp as the sun started to wash away the darkness of the night. As they took stock of the makeshift campsite, Nova saw Aggie; their eyes narrowed. *What are you?* Nova thought.

Aggie looked up in Nova's general direction. "So you're back. Good."

Nova remained silent.

Aggie shrugged. "It's fine. I don't need to be able to see you. Knowing you're here is enough."

Nova moved to kneel behind Ryan; he shifted closer to them, and Nova laid one hand on his shoulder. He settled back into the stillness of sleep. Nova looked down at their first real friend, and for the first time since they were fourteen, Nova cried.

Aggie sat down, her back propped up against her pack. "It's a shame it took you so long to catch up to your friends. You missed a great story of mine." She shrugged as she closed her eyes against the rising sun. "I guess you'll hear about it soon enough."

PART TWO

The Mundane

Mind over matter
Is no matter for me.
When I reach inside
There is fight or flight.
No magic.
Only searing pain
Buried through the years.
Repression is
Your superpower.

Marissa

"Ugh," I groaned. I was not made for outside living. Even after using the supplies we brought with us, my mouth felt gritty, and my hair was a knotted mass that a messy bun only partially fixed. I side-eyed Ryan, who was still sleeping soundly, and I looked around for Aggie. I saw her at the other side of the clearing, and she smiled brightly at me. I resisted a snarl; morning people are all a special brand of evil.

"Good morning!"

"Yeah, yeah," I grumbled as I pushed myself to my feet. I stretched and, to my chagrin, everything inside of me popped like bubble wrap.

"A little stiff?"

"You could say that." I focused my gaze on Aggie and narrowed my eyes. "Why do you look so perfect?"

She chuckled, a deep sound that was so smooth my feathers immediately unruffled. "Practice. When you've lived like a nomad for as long as I have, you learn a few things."

I found myself grinning at her. "Well, I think it's safe to say that the nomadic lifestyle is not for me." I sat down by my pack and started to untangle my coiled mess of hair from the ouch-less hair tie. When I finally managed to break my hair free from the constraints of the band, I grimaced at how much hair had come with the hair band. I sniffed the air, and my insides percolated. "Is that...?"

"The best part of waking up? You bet."

"Goddess."

Aggie faltered suddenly, and coffee sloshed over the edge of her camp mug. Then the moment passed, and she was fine. "Not quite. Just resourceful." After handing me the mug, she started to break camp, meticulously putting everything into her pack. What wasn't hers, she divided into piles. I recognized some of my things I had left out, and Ryan's too, but there was a pile of things I didn't recognize.

"Whose are those?"

Aggie shrugged. "I'm not sure. But they were here when we got here. We should probably divide these things and take them with us. Extra supplies."

It seemed like a good plan, but I worried that whoever's stuff this was would come back. At the same time, *I could definitely use a new giant hoodie,* I rationalized as I picked up the well-worn grey sweatshirt.

Ryan sat up abruptly and started whispering to Nova. I rolled my eyes; they were always doing that. I set my coffee down and continued to finger-detangle my hair.

Ryan came over and sat next to me. "Hey," he said.

"Finally awake, I see."

Ryan leaned hard against my arm, and I felt drain away my frustration at his easy ability to sleep on the hard ground. "Ris, we need to get out of here. Let's go home."

"Finally! That is the first sane thing you've said since this whole crazy trip began."

"Yeah, I know. Sorry. But how are we going to get away from Aggie?"

"DUDE!" My voice was louder than necessary; I dropped it to a whisper. "She saved our asses—"

"Yes, technically, but Nova—"

"Nova abandoned us yesterday to wander the woods. Alone."

"No, they stayed behind to…"

I could see him struggling to remember what he was going to say. I leaned closer for some of his natural comfort. "Listen, it's okay. I know you two have been BFFs or whatever for a really long time, but even you have to admit that they came back from that weird walkabout different."

Ryan hung his head. "I know, but it doesn't change the fact that they're right. It's time to go. And we need to lose Aggie. She doesn't have any color."

I looked incredulously at Ryan. "Any color?"

He looked at me intensely. "Yeah. Color. You know, your color is red, Nova's used to be a pearlescent white, mine is yellow, and…"

"And what?" I prompted.

Ryan shrugged. "I don't know. I just feel like something is not right."

I nodded even though I had zero idea what he was talking about. We fell silent, and I watched Aggie finish packing.

I looked around and marveled. The whole campsite looked as though we had never been there.

Nova dropped down beside me. "Okay, time to go."

"Ris won't come with us."

"What does that mean?" Nova demanded, sounding more freaked out than angry.

I leveled a look at Nova. "It means that you left Ry and me to find our own way back. ALONE! After Aggie finished packing her stuff, she followed Ryan's ribbons—which she gave us to help us not get more lost, by the way—and then she got us closer to civilization than Ryan has managed to since we set foot on this godforsaken trail! While you stayed behind for…what? To *sulk*?"

"Sulk? I stayed behind to take care of John!" Nova cried out and began to sob.

Ryan's head and mine snapped up. "Who?"

"John. Our friend. The person who suggested this doomed trip in the first place. His tattoos kept getting infected; you guys were supposed to go get help. Aggie stayed with John, and I—"

"Kept your distance?" Ryan asked shortly.

"Something like that," Nova said disdainfully. "Anyway, I went to make sure you had marked your trail, but when I got back, John was asleep, and Aggie was hunched over him. Singing."

I shook my head. "Singing? To a friend that only Nova remembers? You want to take their word? You're cracked. I'm getting out of here. With Aggie's help, not yours. You two do whatever you want." I stood up, hauled my pack onto my shoulders, and walked over to Aggie. *Forget those two,* I thought to myself. *I wanted to stay home and study. I never wanted to come on this dumb trip.*

Aggie looked over her shoulder at Ryan. "Where's he going?"

"To hell, I hope. And he better take Nova with him."

Aggie smiled thinly. "Ah, Nova. Well, we can keep heading for the rangers' station, so you can charge your phone, and then they can get you out of here."

"Thank you. Yes."

*

Aggie and I walked all day, and still the elusive rangers' station remained just out of reach. "Girl, I have got to stop."

Aggie frowned but relented. "Yes, okay."

I dropped my pack and chugged some water. *Thank God, Ryan made us buy all that water,* I thought guiltily. *I left them out there. Why do I always do that? Not all bridges need to be burned, especially when I'm still on them.*

Aggie sat on a boulder and leaned back against a tree that had grown right behind it. "We should try to get a little farther. This isn't a great place to stop."

"Aggie, I can't keep going. My feet are killing me."

Aggie huffed a sigh and jumped off the rock. "Fine, but we won't have room for a fire."

I crushed the empty water bottle and glared. "Fine, whatever. I'll layer up. I just want to sleep." I pulled on a few sweatshirts, including the one I had taken that morning. I inhaled deeply. It smelled familiar, but I couldn't place the scent. Finally, I unpacked my bedroll and all but collapsed onto it.

After a tense few minutes, Aggie settled down by my feet. "I'm sorry. I'm not used to traveling with anyone. I've been on my own for a long time."

I rolled onto my back and propped my head up so I could look at her. "Me too."

Aggie nodded. "I could tell that about you. We are kindred spirits, you and I."

Uh-oh, I thought. *Now is not the time to get into this.* "Yeah, I guess." My voice sounded rough to my own ears, and I swallowed hard. "It sucks when your own family doesn't understand you, doesn't it?"

Aggie nodded and pulled her guitar into her lap. "My sisters and I lost contact over something very petty a long time ago. The world is not kind to people like us."

I nodded in agreement. Aggie started strumming and I felt my eyes grow heavy. "We only have ourselves."

"Exactly."

800 BCE

Sister, I implore thee
Stand by my side.
Support me. Stay with me.

*

Anyone watching would have thought that the three sisters stretched out on the sun-cooked rocks were completely oblivious to the foamy white tide inching closer to their pointed talons. To the ship that was sailing dangerously close to their island. That person would be dangerously wrong. Even at rest, the three women watched their island with a keen eye and killer instincts. The Sirens, the guardians of Persephone, had been banished to this island by Demeter.

Since that time, the eldest sister ruled their tiny sanctuary with an iron fist. All rules followed, nothing out of place, and every day the same as the day before, especially when it came time to eat. She sat up on her elbows and opened her crystal-green eyes. "Ladies, we have company."

Following their sister's gaze, the other two spied the ship in the distance. Sun-bleached sails billowed in a wind that would send the ship right to the jagged rocks hidden beneath the water, marooning the sailors. Their fate was sealed. The youngest sister ran her tongue over her fangs and said,

"Thank Persephone for that. I'm dying of hunger. Do you think they're protected?"

"They're too far away to know for sure, but I hope they aren't. Wouldn't it be nice to have a full meal?"

The middle sister, Aglaope, lay back down, her wings spread wide to protect her skin from the heat of the rocks. She threw an arm across her eyes to shield them from the sun. "Well, whoever they are, they sure are brave sailing this way."

Peisinoe looked at her younger sister. "You could be a little more excited. We haven't eaten in weeks."

Aglaope turned her head toward her sister. "*You* haven't eaten in weeks. My last catch lasted me a good long while."

"Why do you keep bragging about that? You know you should have shared him with us. In fact, when we realized how long you'd kept him and hadn't even started to actually eat him until we found you, we should have punished you then and there."

"That's what I've been trying to tell you! We don't—"

"Enough."

Thelxiepeia, the youngest, pulled her white-blonde hair over her shoulder, taking care to make sure the ends weren't tangled in her raven wings, ready once again to mediate between her sisters. "It's done. We've moved on. All I know is that I'm hungry. I can't wait. Can we sing now? Can we?"

Peisinoe smiled placatingly at Thelxiepeia. "They would never hear us from that distance, but there are others who would." She was thinking of Demeter, the scorned goddess who blamed the sisters for Persephone's capture, and of Poseidon, the god who, if he heard them singing before the ship was within the boundaries he set for them, would make sure the sailors were protected, even if they had left port without saying the appropriate prayers. Peisinoe ran her hand over the ribbon of scars on her arm from her last meeting with Demeter. "No, we will wait."

Aglaope sat completely forward and wrapped her arms around her knees. "We could fly to our borders and help them find their way here."

Peisinoe glared at her sister. "Why don't you understand? That's not how this works. We are exiled here because we failed Demeter. This is our punishment."

"To feed on scraps that they deign to allow us?"

"And we should be grateful they allow us to eat at all."

Aglaope turned to Thelxiepeia, who was staring stonily out at the water, avoiding both of her sisters' gazes. "What do you have to say about all of this?"

She shrugged. "There's nothing to say. We are stuck here; we feed whenever we ensnare a ship that was stupid enough to set sail without Poseidon's blessing and to actually sail into our rocks. *And* you two will go on arguing for the rest of eternity."

Aglaope mistook her sister's anger for sadness that she and Peisinoe were fighting again. She wrapped her arm around Thelxiepeia's shoulders. "I'm sorry. We'll stop fighting. We don't mean to upset you."

Thelxiepeia pushed her sister's arm off and stood up. "I'm hot. I'm going in. Tell me when I need to come out and watch for the ship." She stormed into the cave where they slept, leaving her sisters in a stony silence.

*

Raise your voices!
Take back your power!
Exile be damned!
We are the rulers of this realm.

*

In the days that followed, the sisters took turns keeping watch on the ship. The argument had left the sisters not speaking. Aglaope welcomed the silence. She resented being tethered to this ridiculous rock that everyone had the audacity to call an island. If it were an island, there would be some sign of life other than the other two Harpies with which she was strapped to it. *Ha, Harpies.* Aglaope chuckled to herself. If her sisters had heard that comparison, she probably would have been given much worse than just the silent treatment.

Aglaope looked out at the ship. She tucked her curling hair behind her ear. Her sisters were sleeping, and the ship was *so* close. She could lure it closer; all she had to do was fly a little bit outside of their borders. It had been so long since she had flown.

She looked over her shoulder to the cave where her sisters lay in their nests built from the bones of sailors. What was the point in waiting any longer? Before Aglaope could talk herself out of this dangerous move, she climbed to the highest point of the island and curled her toes over the cliff's edge. Aglaope spread her arms and felt her wings follow suit. Goddess, it felt good to stretch her wings all the way out.

Since being banished to the island, Peisinoe hadn't let them do anything with their wings other than pad their nests with the feathers they shed. Flying was out of the question because the temptation to leave their territory was too great. Peisinoe had assured the upper echelons that they could control themselves and would never fly again.

As Aglaope stood feeling the wind push against her wings and threaten to knock her down, she didn't know how she had managed to resist this so long. Aglaope pushed back against the wind and answered the call of the sky. She stepped off the cliff's edge, a scream lodged in her throat as she dove. Just as her fingers touched the surface of the sea, instinct took over and she rocketed above the clouds. She had missed this kind of freedom.

With a grin frozen to her face, she descended and spotted her quarry. The ship's oars slapped the water rhythmically. Hovering above the mast, Aglaope swayed in time with each splash of the sea and slice of the oars. Slowly, she started to sing. It was a wordless tune that kept the oarsmen rowing and put to sleep everyone else within earshot. Finishing her song, Aglaope stretched into a long barrel roll and soared back to the island, knowing the ship would be stuck by morning.

*

Hear me! Let me
Lead the way! No! Please don't
Turn your backs.
I give you everything and
Am met
With silence.

*

Just as the sun crested the horizon, the ship became wedged on the rocks in the shallows surrounding the island. Aglaope shouted, "Sisters! They are here! Sisters!" She heard the clacking of bones hitting against each other as her sisters rose from their nests and made their way slowly out of the cave.

"What?" Peisinoe asked, rubbing her eyes and shielding them from the morning's sun.

Thelxiepeia stretched her feathered arms toward the sky, and her wings stretched out to her sides. "How did they get here so fast?"

The lie was quick on Aglaope's tongue. "The wind was strong last night."

Peisinoe eyed her younger sister suspiciously. "Well, let's go see what we've got."

As the sisters boarded the ship, Aglaope noted that, while it was an older ship, it was still very well cared for. The warship was well traveled, its sails mended several times and the wooden decks worn shiny with regular walking and swabbing. "This is a trireme," Aglaope said to no one in particular.

"A what?" Peisinoe asked.

"A trireme. That's what these types of warships are called." Aglaope shrugged, as though it were something that everyone knew.

Peisinoe slowly turned to face Aglaope. "How do you know that?"

Aglaope shrugged. "You eat enough sailors, you learn things."

"Aglaope? Were you on deck before us?" Thelxiepeia asked coldly.

Peisinoe and Aglaope turned from their face-off and saw Thelxiepeia slowly running a dove-grey feather through her skeletal fingers.

"Was I—"

"What. Did. You. Do," Peisinoe demanded, eyes flashing.

Aglaope clenched her fists at her sides. "I did what I had to do."

"Oh…oh…what *you* had to do? That's what it always is, isn't it? *You* had to bring the ship in. *You* had to keep a meal. *You* had to keep Persephone's secret. What do *you* think would have happened if Poseidon had heard *you*?"

"If he had heard me? Well, I guess *you* would be down a sister."

Peisinoe took a step forward and grabbed Aglaope's arm. "Is that what you think? That he would just kill you? *Only* you? Do you even know what I had to—"

"Hello? Is someone up there?"

Both sisters started at the faint voice from beneath their feet. "What the Hades was that?" Peisinoe whispered harshly.

"How should I know?" Aglaope wrenched her arm free and looked for where a trapdoor might be.

"Um, I think that we've hit some rocks. Water is filling the brig."

Aglaope found the door and yanked hard.

Peisinoe stood by, fuming. "Why isn't he under your spell?"

"I was singing quietly. I didn't want to wake anyone." All at once, the trapdoor gave way, and Aglaope tumbled backwards on the deck.

A man crawled out of the brig, dripping seawater all over Aglaope's feet. "Wow, thank you. I didn't think any—" He stopped abruptly as he realized that his saviors were not saviors at all. "Sirens!" the man exclaimed as he turned and ran.

*

I watch from the sun-bleached
Sand as my sisters partake
Then play in the surf.
I am on the outside.

*

It didn't take long for the Sirens to ravage the ship. Peisinoe took the officers on deck, while Thelxiepeia took the oarsmen. Peisinoe told Aglaope that, as punishment, she couldn't have anyone on the ship, but she could have the man who got away…if she could catch him.

Aglaope didn't mind. She still wasn't hungry after her last meal, and the prisoner hiding on their rock wasn't a problem. There were only so many places he could hide, and any other land was days away. No human could swim that distance and survive.

Aglaope sat on the rocky beach and slowly finger-combed her salt-crusted hair; every so often, she hit a tangle, but she just patiently combed through her hair until all the wind snarls were gone. Aglaope pulled her knees to her chin and wrapped herself in her wings. It was true that Aglaope had kept that other man a secret, but she'd learned something that could keep her sisters alive and full for so much longer than just stripping the meat from the bones and eating it.

If they would just listen to me.

By accident, Aglaope had discovered the secret to taking someone's mind. She had been singing to keep her quarry enthralled and weak so that she could tie him up and take her time eating him. She always started with the toes; they were the worst part, so she got that over with first and then worked her way up. This time, though, something new happened.

She let her mind wander as she sang, and then visions filled her mind—the first time he had manned the sails, the feel of the sea spray on his face, his mother smiling and waiting at the dock for his return from sea... Aglaope stopped singing, sat down, and looked at the man. For the first time since she and her sisters were banished, her hunger was completely sated.

It was through that man's visions that she had learned how ships work, what the different types of ships were called, and how to navigate beyond her small island and small slice of the sea. Life. There was life out there, and she wanted to taste it all. She hadn't meant to keep him a secret. She just wanted something that was just hers, but she knew she had to tell her sisters about what she discovered. Before Aglaope could tell them, though, they found the sailor and forced her to kill him and eat the flesh from his bones.

She was still on the beach and lost in thought when her sisters returned. They were in much better spirits, laughing and splashing in the surf, trying to rinse off all the blood. Behind them, the boat was engulfed in flames.

"Hey, why didn't you go catch your meal?" Thelxiepeia called out.

Aglaope smiled at her younger sister. "I wasn't hungry." She looked pointedly at Peisinoe.

Peisinoe stood up, her golden-blonde hair streaming down her body, dripping rivulets of water down her thighs. "You'll probably still be too full when the next ship comes. Why don't you leave that one to us too."

Thelxiepeia said, "Why do you have to treat each other that way? It's so unnecessary." She stormed out of the surf, wringing the salty water out of the ends of her sun-bleached hair.

"What? She could have starved us to death by not sharing that last one."

Aglaope stood up. "If you would listen to me, you would know that—"

"I don't want to hear any more about this. You kept a secret from us, and I am allowed to punish you as I see fit."

"Because you are the eldest."

"Yes, dammit, because I am the oldest. It is my job to keep us alive!" Peisinoe still stood in the knee-deep water as she screamed at Aglaope.

"And it doesn't matter to you if I might have found a better way to do that…to help us?"

Peisinoe crossed her arms over her chest and stormed to shore. "No, our ways are fine the way that they are. It has worked for decades, and will continue to work long after I have decided you have been punished enough." She strode into the cave to sulk.

Aglaope sat on the shore long after the sun sank below the horizon. Finally, sighing, she stood, brushed the gravel off her legs and feet, and started to walk. Even though she wasn't hungry yet, she should find the man sooner, rather than later, so that it wouldn't be a mad dash to find him when she *was* hungry. This way, she could incapacitate him and keep him until she was ready.

Aglaope was on her third trip around the craggy perimeter when it hit her. The sharp tang of fear. It was a smell unlike any other; it made the air swell, and it always lingered long after she and her sisters had finished eating the men who were brave enough to face the unknown of the seas, but who, when faced with the three sisters, would cry to Zeus for help. She forced her breathing to slow to almost nothing.

Aglaope found him cowering behind a small pile of rocks; her lips curved cruelly. *What will I learn from this one?*

*

Maybe I belong
Alone.
My sisters are two
And I am
My own monster.

*

Every night, Aglaope waited until her sisters were sleeping before she crept out of the cave and made her way to the rocks where she was keeping the man. She smiled to herself as she rifled through the memories of his that she had taken. There was a lot to gain from him, and it was fun to watch him strain for memories that now belonged to her. In fact, the night before, she'd ended her song, looked at him, and asked, "So…did you leave any family behind before stowing away on the ship?" She watched him struggle for several minutes, his growing anxiety making her want to sing again, but she didn't want to go too fast; she might lose him altogether.

This night, she came to the rocks, watched him for a few moments, and saw that he was sitting completely still, looking at nothing. Curiously, she crept closer and realized he wasn't going to respond to her at all. She kneeled in front of him and saw blood pooling in his lap; it had poured from a gaping wound across his throat.

"Damnation."

"Are you surprised that we found your newest secret?"

Aglaope whirled around.

Peisinoe and Thelxiepeia stood up from their hiding spot. "How dare you keep another one from us."

"You said that I could have this one if I could catch him. I caught him; he was mine to do with what I pleased."

"I meant you could eat if you found him. Not keep him as a pet."

Aglaope looked up at her sister. "He wasn't a pet. He was feeding me. And feeding me well. He could have fed all of us, but I knew you wouldn't listen to me!"

"About what? A new way to do things. You can't keep doing things *your* way. That's what got us banished! You! *You* wanted to side with Persephone! It was her mother that assigned us to her; we were to report everything. But there you were, staying silent when Persephone was planning to run away."

Aglaope stood, staring agog at her sister. "You mean planning to have her own life outside of the one with her mother and Zeus? I still don't even know how Demeter found out what was happening! Thank the gods that Hades came for her early!"

"It wasn't your choice to make to keep that from Persephone's mother! We were in *her* employ, not her daughter's! It is for you to follow what the gods tell us to do."

"Not. Anymore."

Peisinoe moved to Aglaope's side with unnatural speed and yanked her to her feet. "You will mind me. Or you will be banished."

Peisinoe and Thelxiepeia pulled Aglaope away from the sailor's body and hauled her back to their cave. Once they were inside their cave, Peisinoe and Thelxiepeia shoved Aglaope down onto her nest, its bones biting into her skin.

Aglaope pushed herself into a sitting position and looked at her sisters. "Please, I beg of you. I know you both feel betrayed, but if you would just listen."

This time it was Thelxiepeia who spoke. "No, I'm done with the fighting. Peisinoe asked you for one thing. To kill and eat. You never listen."

Aglaope's mouth fell open. Thelxiepeia never spoke to her that way; she never spoke to anyone that way. "Sister, I am sorry you feel this way."

"No. No more false apologies. You have taken matters into your own hands too often. You are banished."

Peisinoe couldn't believe what she just heard. "Thelxiepeia! That is not for you to decide!"

Aglaope stood and faced her sisters. "No, she's right. I don't belong here anymore. I'll leave tomorrow at sunset. I'll let the sea decide my fate, as do the travelers that visit us."

Peisinoe nodded. "We will see you off then."

*

My blood coats
Their hands. Stains
That can never by washed away.
Sisters no more.
I raise my voice.
Hear my song!

*

Aglaope stood on the edge of the island, looking into the sunset. "Red sky at night, sailor's delight." She sighed, suddenly very sad. The island had never been her home; her home was her sisters. Aglaope wished that she could stay, that she could make her sisters understand how much more than just meat they could get from what they caught.

She sighed again as Thelxiepeia came to stand beside her. "Come with me," Aglaope said. "We'll leave together. Start a new life."

Thelxiepeia crossed her arms over her chest and looked at her older sister. "You don't get it, do you?"

"Get what?"

"You did this. You got us put on this rock, and now we're just supposed to let you go? Do you know what will happen to you out there?"

Aglaope pushed her hair behind her ear. "Well, I'm assuming that Demeter or Poseidon will kill me before I even reach land, but I have to try. I can't stay here anymore. I want to fly."

Thelxiepeia nodded. "Oh, you want to *fly*?"

Her sister's voice had taken on an edge that she'd never heard before. Aglaope took a step back before replying, "Yes, I want to fly."

Peisinoe appeared behind her and pinned Aglaope's arms to her sides.

"Get her down on the ground." Thelxiepeia had pulled a sharpened stone from behind her back.

Peisinoe wrestled Aglaope facedown on the rocks.

Aglaope fought to lift her face from the burning-hot stone. "Please, sisters, what are you doing?"

Thelxiepeia kneeled next to her head and put her face close to Aglaope's. "What needs to be done." She then grabbed one of Aglaope's wings and began to saw at its base with the stone.

Aglaope writhed and screamed over the sound of sawing. Peisinoe's grip loosened, and Aglaope got an arm free.

"I said you would need to hold her tight. Now do it!"

Peisinoe shifted so that her knee was braced on Aglaope's back; her other leg was planted firmly on the rock. Peisinoe twisted Aglaope's wayward arm back under control.

As Thelxiepeia continued to hack at the wing, Aglaope's screams subsided into sobbing. She pressed the side of her face into the rocks as she watched feathers fall around her. By the time Thelxiepeia had finished with the first wing, Aglaope was completely numb.

The silent acceptance made Peisinoe nauseous.

Aglaope could see her sister's bloodstained hair, which hung down and swung with the rhythm of the sawing. She could feel the pressure of Peisinoe's hands on her wrists and the knee that was holding her down. None of it mattered. She had accepted her death as inevitable when she made the decision to leave the island; there was no way the gods would let her survive past the boundaries they had set. This, though, was a fate worse than death. Knowing the true hatred her sisters harbored for her. Knowing they were deliberately taking away her last flight.

Thelxiepeia stood up, threw the second wing on the ground, and looked down at her sisters. "Throw her in the sea."

Peisinoe let go of Aglaope's arms and stood to face her baby sister. "What?"

"Throw her in. I'm going to get cleaned up. I don't want to see her when I get back." Thelxiepeia walked away.

Peisinoe kneeled back beside Aglaope and stroked her back through the blood. "I am so sorry. She convinced me that doing this would keep you safe from the gods. I know now that I was wrong. So very wrong."

Aglaope rolled onto her side and cradled one of her wings. "It's done."

Peisinoe rubbed her sticky fingers on the rocks to clean away the blood. "Yes, well…"

Aglaope slowly got to her feet and dropped her wing. Peisinoe reached for her, but Aglaope held up a hand. "Please. Don't. I will put myself into the sea if you don't mind. You can tell Thelxiepeia anything you want, but allow me this."

Peisinoe took a step back to give her sister some space to ease herself into the sea. She saw Aglaope shudder as the salty water reached the gaping wounds where her wings had been and felt ill as blood stained the water.

Aglaope allowed her body to float out to sea with the current.

Peisinoe stood watching and said a quick protection prayer to Amphitrite to keep her sister safe.

MARISSA

"Well, I guess that's everything," I said, tucking my hands in my pockets and hoping that my aunt wouldn't want another hug.

She did. Aunt Paula pulled me in tight and whispered in my hair, "Your parents would be so proud of you."

I nodded and swallowed hard around the rock of grief that formed whenever they were mentioned. I untangled myself from my aunt's grasp and smiled tightly. "Thanks for everything. I mean it."

Aunt Paula pulled her bandana off her mass of curly hair, which so closely resembled my own, to wipe away her tears. "You're sure you want to drive all that way by yourself?"

"Auntie"—I rolled my eyes—"it's time to go. It's a long drive."

"Of course. I just love you so much. Please call me. And text me every time you stop."

I started climbing into my Jeep, but she just kept talking.

"And share your location with me."

I pulled the door shut harder than I needed to, and when I turned to apologize, I found Aunt Paula gripping the door and shoving her face through the open window. "Whoa! Auntie!"

"I know. Just one more thing." She handed me a small pocket-knife. "Keep this in your shoe. At all times."

"Jesus! You already gave me pepper spray, both on a key chain and disguised as a lipstick. And a blowhorn that fits in my back-pack. Now a knife?!" But I slid the knife into my shoe anyway, and when I sat up, I was in the passenger seat watching myself say goodbye.

"Why don't you text her more?"

I shook my head at myself. "I'm going to as soon as I wake up. Auntie deserves better."

I had had lucid dreams as long as I could remember, so I relaxed back in the passenger seat and smiled as my past dream self searched our iPod for the perfect start-off-to-college song.

I started to hum along, only to realize that the song I remembered settling on was not what was coming through my speakers. Instead of the female-led metal jam, it was a slow, eerie ballad. As the Jeep started forward, the music got louder.

I opened my eyes; that was Aggie's voice singing about betrayal and sisterhood. It filled the air around me, and I struggled to hear anything else. I turned in my seat to look back at Aunt Paula, but behind me there was only grey fog.

"HEY!" I screamed. I turned to look at myself, who—I remembered too late—had turned the music up all the way to cover the sounds of my sobbing. The feeling of being alone came flooding back. I felt so alone in that moment, and it sucked.

I faced forward again; the road was gone. I was completely encased in grey fog. I had to get out of here. I took a chance and *leapt from the Jeep. I landed hard and rolled, but what I landed on was as nondescript as the grey by which I was surrounded.*

I ran back in the direction that I thought my aunt had been standing and screamed, "NO! Where are you?"

*

I sat up, tears streaming down my face. "What's happening?"

Aggie, too, sat up and scrubbed at her eyes, as though she had been sleeping. "What's wrong?"

I reached down to my boot, but as my hand slid to my shoe—empty!—I couldn't for the life of me figure out why I would do that.

"Is your foot okay?" Aggie asked, grinning.

I shook my head, trying to clear the fog that had settled in hard. "Yeah, it's fine. This is going to sound weird, but I thought I needed something in there."

Aggie's grin stretched into laughter. "In your boot? What could you possibly keep in there, other than your foot?" Her voice was mocking and harsh, and I was hurt. I mean, I knew she was mad when we had to stop yesterday, but was she really still so angry at me today? I decided that I was hearing things and that my weird grey dream had left me more disoriented than I thought.

I shrugged and busied myself reorganizing my pack. "Another long day of walking ahead of us?"

"Probably not. I mean, you know how tired you get."

I glared at her. "Listen, I didn't want to come on this stupid trip anyway. It was all…" I hesitated; I couldn't remember whose idea the trip had been.

"All what?"

"Never mind. Let's just get out of this hellscape so I can take my friends back to school, graduate, and move on."

"The friends that left you alone with a stranger?"

"Don't speak about them that way. They are the first real friends I've had since my parents died."

Aggie held up her hands in surrender. "Fine. I just think it's strange."

I turned my back to her, forced my sleeping bag and bedroll into the semblance of a cylinder, and yanked on the straps, not caring anymore if it actually fit. "Let's get out of here." I stood and swung my pack onto my back, staggering a little under its weight.

*

My phone died when we stopped for lunch. I was trying to respond to a text from my aunt in which she asked if I had asked John out yet. I had just finished typing, "Who is John?" when the screen went black. "Dammit."

Aggie shook her head. "Technology. So useful. Until it isn't."

I grimaced. "Please, I've had enough. If you don't want to help me anymore, just point me in the direction of the rangers' station, and I'll be gone."

Aggie sighed heavily and raked her head with the sharpest-looking nails I'd ever seen. "No, I'm sorry. I've been on my own for a very long time. I have forgotten how to be with people, I think."

I laughed sadly. "Well, I've never really known how to be with people, so at least you knew at one point."

Aggie came and plopped down next to me. "Don't you wish you could just forget it all? All the pain? Anger? Everything?"

"Right now, all I want to do is get to a phone charger. My aunt is probably freaking out because I haven't texted her back yet."

Aggie pulled a bag of turkey jerky from the side pocket of my pack, handed it to me, and said, "Then let's get moving."

*

As the sun went down, I stared at the station. We were so close, and I had made it farther than I did the day before. "A little bit ahead, there's a small clearing; I've used it before. We'll stop there. Okay?"

I wanted to push on; something was telling me that I had to call Aunt Paula. The blisters on my feet were telling me that I needed to stop, though. "Thanks."

Aggie nodded and jostled me with a smile. "I promise this epic trek will end soon." She continued walking ahead on the trail.

"It better." I jiggled the keys in my hoodie pocket. They were lighter than I thought they should be. "I swear to God, if

I lost a key…" I pulled the key chain free and counted, "Jeep. Apartment. Storage." Nope, they were all there, and yet… something was definitely missing. I slowly raised and lowered my hand, testing their weight. "Why can't I remember?"

"Hmm?" Aggie turned back. "Did you ask me something?"

"You ever feel as though you'd misplaced something, but you have no idea what it could be?"

"I don't have enough to misplace anything."

"Yeah, I guess."

Aggie shrugged awkwardly, and her shawl slipped. A feather gently wafted to the ground.

"Hey! You dropped something!" I picked up the enormous feather and smiled broadly. "Maybe I should call you Owl Lady."

Aggie pulled up short and lifted her eyes to mine. "What. Did. You. Say?"

I held up the feather that had fallen from Aggie's shawl and said apprehensively, "This looks like a barn-owl feather—a huge one, but still… Anyway, this fell out of your shawl, and I said we should call you Owl Lady. I'm sorry. I didn't mean to make you mad again. You must have picked this up in your travels without realizing it."

Aggie closed her eyes and sighed. It looked as if she was forcing herself to relax. "It's fine. You're right. I must have picked it up somewhere." She slid her golden pin out of the fabric, pulled her shawl tighter, and slid the brooch back into place, all the while taking slow, calculated breaths.

I dropped the feather. "I can't wait to see what falls out of my bag when I get home."

"Or what you've dropped."

I laughed nervously and changed the subject. "How far did you say we had to go?"

Aggie gestured broadly behind her. "This far."

I stopped. "Wait. We're back where we started?"

Aggie looked at me and then back at the clearing. "What? No. It must just look like that to you because you don't camp much. There must be hundreds of little hideaway sites like this all over the Pacific Crest Trail. Come on. Let's set up for the night."

In the time it took me to get my bedroll and sleeping bag set up, Aggie had a fire going and dinner made. I was so tired that I took the sandwich she offered and ate it lying down. I brushed the crumbs off my chest, pillowed my head in my arms, and watched the embers float toward the sky.

"Marissa, I'm sorry about my reaction before. It's been a long time since I was called Owl Lady."

I rolled onto my side to face her. In the firelight, Aggie's face had taken on an unearthly glow. "Why were you called Owl Lady?"

Aggie smiled sadly and started to rub her hands on her jeans. The rhythmic sound was soothing, and my eyes grew heavy.

1200

The man hurried down the moonlit paths, hunched under the weight of his bulging sack. He knew his way home, but he was grateful for the silvery light, lest he cross paths with someone who wished to relieve him of his newest treasure.

*

In the misty frost
I was captured.
He said I was his Fate.
That may be so.
But he is not mine.

*

I had been hearing the mournful singing for days, ever since the Wise Man returned one hazy morning, bent under the weight of his newest trade. I was skeptical since he had left town with only his owl staff and wearing his finest sunset-blue robes, but he returned only a few days later with all those possessions, plus a giant sack that had feathers poking out all over it.

Each day, the Wise Man pushed open his shutters, drew deeply on his pipe, raised his hands, and said a prayer to the dawn. I leaned on my broom for a time and watched him. Once he turned his back on the window, I returned to my chores and waited for him to emerge.

His door creaked open, and out the Wise Man shuffled out. It always made me smile because I knew it was an act. He was much more spry than he seemed. When I first came to Caerleon, in response to my "Good morning," the Wise Man just stared at me and ran his knobby fingers through his long beard, which was always tucked into his belt. I thought he might be mute, but I continued to wish him a good morning daily anyway.

Finally, one day, he crossed to where I swept every morning, squinted at me, said, "No, not yet," and went on his way into the fog that bordered the land.

That exchange became our whole relationship. I waved and called out, "Good morning!" and he crossed over to me, squinted into my face, and said, "No, not yet."

Then came the day he returned with the bulging sack on his back. He stopped, still carrying the bag, smiled, and said, "Ah, we're getting closer now."

Closer? Closer to what? I didn't know.

My guardian, Sir Hector, warned me that the Wise Man was no one to be trifled with because he was the only person who could navigate the white wall of mist that edged our land. I nodded now, remembering when I first started working for Sir Hector. I pouted about all of the chores; I was expected to sweep, polish, and be a servant. That wasn't how I had been treated in my family's home. How would I ever learn to be a knight this way?

I decided that I had had enough; I threw my broom down on the ground and walked to the mist wall. Without hesitation, I stepped forward and immediately regretted my decision. I was overcome by complete disorientation. I felt as though I were drowning and collapsed under the weight of the fog.

The Wise Man found me sobbing and brought me back to our village. He stood me up, handed me my broom, and then walked away shaking his head. I went straight back to my chores, praying that Sir Hector hadn't noticed I was missing.

Sir Hector was a giant compared to my scrawny thirteen-year-old self. He towered over me, and although he spoke gently with the people in the town, with me he was gruff, harsh, and oftentimes plain mean. I'm sure it was to toughen me up for when I was finally able to join the knighthood, but when he dropped armor into my arms and then just stood there as I buckled under its weight, I hated him. So much so that the day I went into the mist I was sure it was my time to be free. But it turned out to be a nightmare worse than anything Hector could rain down on my head. So I stuck it out, and swept, polished, and moved armor from one place to another.

And it started to get easier.

Until the day I listened to the music.

I had been hearing it for some time, but I hadn't ever stopped to really listen to it. When I stopped sweeping and looked around, I noticed that the activity on the whole street had paused. People were frozen midstride; a woman in a building across the way was stuck holding an overturned bucket. The only ones unaffected by the song were the animals pulling the carts.

What was happening? With every breath I took, I felt as though I were breathing under water; my limbs grew heavy, and I felt my eyes close as I rested my forehead against the broom.

*

I trace my time
By the movement of
Helios and his Sky Chariot.
One prison for another.
One cage for another.

*

When I surfaced from the haze, I knew I had to find the source of the song. I set my broom by the front door of Sir Hector's armory and strode to the Wise Man's house. At the door, I lost my nerve. What if there wasn't anything in there? What if it was all in my mind? Did I really want to risk everything I had worked for?

The singing started again; it was such a mournful sound.

I steeled myself and pushed open the door. As silently as I could, I crept through the Wise Man's house. In the dim, dusty light, I looked around. The house was bare. There was a table with one chair, a wash basin on another table, and under the stairs there was a simple pallet where, I assumed, the Wise Man slept. I made my way to the stairs and started to climb.

The singing was louder at the top of the stairs, but muffled because the door at the top of the stairs was tightly closed. I pushed gently, expecting it to be locked. But it gave way under my hands. I leaned more heavily on it; the hinges groaned as the door swung inward.

My eyes immediately fell upon a massive golden cage. Within its bars was a creature the likes of which I had never seen. Lithe, golden, and hair the color of corn silk. My eyes traveled down her body, and my mouth fell open; her arms had feathers growing from them. Her legs were scaly and rough, like those of a chicken.

"Well? Have you seen enough?" Her voice was harsh, bordering on cruel, but it pulled me from my reverie.

I yanked the door shut and fled back to the safety of my work.

*

A change in the wind.
A strong mind, amidst the sheep.
My captor and I both recognize it.
The steel is coming.

*

Over the next several days, I tried to ignore the singing, but I kept finding myself sweeping to the rhythm she sang out to me. I knew she was singing to me because I was the only one who seemed fazed by it. I watched the people in the street and focused on their footsteps to keep myself grounded in reality. That strange bird-woman up there was trying to get something; obviously, the Wise Man was keeping her locked up for a reason.

Smash!

"Boy! You cannot just stand there and while the day away."

I rubbed the knot in the shape of a jousting glove that was forming at the back of my head. "I'm sorry, milord. I didn't realize I had stopped working."

"Well, now you shall work through supper."

"Supper? But that's hours away!"

Sir Hector scrubbed his face with his hands as though I were an idiot. "Insufferable boy! Look at the horizon! The sun is lowering even as we speak."

I couldn't believe it! I had just started my chores! And now the day was over! I would have to work all night to catch up. "My apologies, milord. It won't happen again."

"It had better not." He stormed away muttering about ungrateful pages.

The next day, I stuffed rags into my ears, and though I could still hear the infernal notes, it didn't have the same effect on me. Even though I felt heavy and foggy all day, I was able to complete my chores. However, I had to do each chore with purpose. Previously, mucking out the stables was a mindless job; now, every stab of the pitchfork felt strange and awkward. Even though I knew I was getting stronger, the pieces of armor, which Sir Hector had set out for me to move, felt heavier than ever, and I had to concentrate because if I dropped one piece, someone could get hurt. Or, worse, a piece of armor could become dented.

*

Vibrations in the air.
Change is coming.
Are they ready for what
The steel is bringing?

*

Days went by, and finally I couldn't take it anymore. No more singing. No more brutality from my master knight. No more fog. I was finished.

So I waited. It wasn't easy; the Wise Man rarely left his house of late, and Sir Hector was preparing for a tournament. However, luck was on my side because Sir Hector finished his tournament preparations early that day and took himself off to the tavern, and the Wise Man hurried into the mist. I looked up and down the abandoned street and raced back to the gilded cage.

"So," the Owl Lady said while baring her pearly fangs, "you've returned. Come to gawk again? Didn't get your fill last time?"

"Not in the slightest. I have come to ask that you stop your incessant singing." I looked straight in her eyes, forcing my gaze not to drop to her bird legs or the pile of giant feathers gathered at her feet.

Her eyes narrowed, and she slid off her bench swing, the claws at the ends of her toes clicking one by one as they touched the floor of the cage. She walked to the edge of the cage and curled black talons around the bars. "You'd like me to what?" She tilted her head to one side and ran her tongue around her sharp teeth.

I took a small step back and swallowed hard. "To…" The words wouldn't come any further; they wrapped themselves like a vise around the knob at the front of my throat.

She nodded, and her ratty hair swung around her shoulders. "Just as I suspected. Another coward. You're all cowards." Turning, she settled back on her swing.

Something about the venomous words had my back up. My shoulders dropped, I lifted my chin proudly, and I stepped all the way up to the cage. "I am telling you to stop singing. It is keeping me from my work."

She kicked her scaly feet out to set herself in motion. "Well, maybe the old man is right about you." She looked thoughtfully at me. "I will stop singing…for a price."

"I have no money," I lied, thinking about the money my family sent to Sir Hector regularly.

She laughed. "We both know that's a lie, but I'll keep your secret."

I was getting angry. "Then what is your price, Owl Lady?"

"Let me sing to you, only to you, one last time."

I hesitated. The last time I listened to her, I had lost almost a full day of memory and then a night's worth of sleep to catch up on all the work I hadn't done. "Why?"

"You have knowledge. I live for knowledge."

"Of what?"

"Of how to get out of here. Of how to get away from that old man. Of the mist."

I shook my head. "Listen, I don't know what you think I know, but I don't even know how the Wise Man got this cage up here."

The Owl Lady leveled a look at me that froze me to the spot. "Trust me, you know more than you think you do."

My stomach dropped to my knees. "I do?"

"You'd be surprised what people aren't conscious of." She started to hum, and I felt the fog rolling in.

"What are you?"

"A memory."

*

And the steel glowed
As He who would be King
Presented it to his people in
The blinding light of the midday sun.

*

I woke the next morning with a strange buzzing in my ears. Something was happening! Hurriedly, I pulled my clothes on and ran outside. The Wise Man was standing at the edge of the mist that bordered our land, running his hands down his beard. In front of him was a boulder, a sword sheathed within it.

The Wise Man caught my eye and smiled mischievously.

The buzzing in my head grew louder, and I started forward.

A giant hand landed hard on my shoulder and yanked me backward. "Where do you think you're going, boy?"

I looked at the man who had taken me in and raised me. He suddenly seemed smaller to me. "I am going to pull that sword from the stone."

Sir Hector threw his head back and laughed, his shoulders rolling with each booming sound. "You? A meek Pendragon?"

"You will not call me meek for long, sir," I sneered.

Sir Hector laughed again. "You know what? Go ahead. You try."

I met the Wise Man's gaze again, and a strange confidence grew within me. "Sir Hector, you will regret laughing at me."

I strode toward the boulder; it was almost as tall as I. After nodding at the Wise Man, I said, "I believe this is here for me, Wise Man."

"I believe you are correct." He bowed and stepped out of the way.

I climbed onto the boulder, my feet fitting in the crevices as though they had been carved just for me, and gripped the hilt of the sword. It warmed in my hands. I barely had to pull for the sword to come loose.

The Wise Man clasped his hands together joyously. "Long Live the King! King Arthur!"

The crowd that had gathered swarmed the boulder and hoisted me onto their shoulders. Over their heads, I watched as a strange woman with feathers on her arms and the legs of an owl walked into the mist.

MARISSA

*T*he white linen brushed my knee in the table fort. I smiled. I loved making forts until...

"No, no. Why am I here?" I folded my legs under me, hunched on my knees, and looked around until I saw her.

Me. Eight years old.

I fell back on my butt and swallowed hard. I was so small. I hadn't felt small. My dad always told me that I was his dragon and fierce enough to rule the whole world. Forts were where I hid my hoard. I leaned over to look in Mini-Me's lap, and then I remembered. No hoard today.

"Well, of course, Paula is going to take her! She's all the family that poor child has left."

"But she's just so...odd. Are you sure—"

A throat cleared, and I smiled. No one messed with Aunt Paula.

"Excuse me. I just need to slide...right...through...here." A slim hand with blue oval nails appeared under the cloth.

Mini-Me took the plate and ate silently as tears splashed the edge of the ivory ceramic. I never questioned how Aunt Paula knew that I was under that table, but I was always grateful for that plate of lemon crinkle cookies and cheese crackers. I felt my own tears start to threaten as I remembered that was the last time that I ate *either of those foods. After the funeral, I couldn't even stand the sight of lemonade; my grief was so deep.*

*

My dream folded into grey, and then I was standing over Aunt Paula while she slept. I smiled softly. She slept with me for months after I moved in with her; I didn't even have to ask her. She just knew it was what I needed. But then I told her I didn't need her to sleep with me anymore; Aunt Paula must have been so hurt, but she stopped. Because I asked her to.

"Why did I ever say I didn't need you anymore?" I said into the silence of my dream. I bent down to kiss her cheek, but she had dissolved into mist.

I straightened. This wasn't right. What was I doing here? "WAKE UP!" I screamed.

I whirled around as I heard a sound from behind me. Singing. Aggie's singing. As the song intensified, another vision rushed toward me. "No! I can't see another memory!" I squeezed my eyes shut so that all I could see was the kaleidoscope behind my eyes, but Aggie's song was piercing my brain.

I clamped my hands over my ears, fell to my knees, and screamed.

*

"Marissa! Wake up!"

I came to abruptly; someone was shaking my shoulders. "What are you doing to me?" I screamed as I wrenched myself out of Aggie's grasp. This wasn't right. None of this was right. I had gaps in my brain. That couldn't be right. Something was wrong with me.

Aggie grabbed ahold of me again as I struggled to get away. "What do you mean? I'm keeping you safe, remember? I'm the one who's going to get you out of here!"

I screamed, "Let me go!" I knew I wasn't safe with her. I stomped on her boot, hard.

She stumbled back, and her shawl fell. I gaped as I saw that her arms were covered in patches of large feathers.

"What are you?"

Aggie's whole demeanor changed, and she glared at me. "I am everything you were warned about when you came out here." She smiled cruelly.

I turned to run, but my foot caught on a root. I fell hard, hit my head on a rock, and then everything went grey.

*

I sat up.

I was alone.

Why?

Why was I in the woods…alone?

Where were all the people?

I pushed to my feet, and the world tilted around me. I pressed the heel of my hand to my head. "Ouch!" I looked at my hand; it was covered in blood.

"What the hell is happening here?"

"Time to run! You have to run! Now!"

"What?" I looked around. "Who's there?"

"Get moving! She's coming back!"

I ran.

Branches snapped overhead, and my feet slid on the unfamiliar terrain. *Where the hell am I? Why am I out here?*

I had to stop; my head was pounding, and I couldn't regain any equilibrium because I was so dizzy. When my breathing evened out, I realized I could hear someone else breathing near me.

"Hello?"

Silence.

"Seriously? Hello!"

"Get. Your. Keys," a voice wheezed in my ear.

"My what?"

"Jeep. Keys! Let's go! Ryan is waiting for us! And she is coming!"

I pulled a set of keys from my hoodie pocket and stared. *Whose keys are these? What is happening to me?*

A hand on my arm pulled me forward. *"Let's go!"*

I didn't need any more prompting. I took off, but in the opposite direction from the one the ghost, or whatever that voice was, was trying to get me to go. There was no way I was going to follow some invisible voice. No trickster was going to get me. I could hear the voice calling after me, but I set my jaw and kept moving away from the voice.

Still, though, I was being followed.

Hunted.

From above.

I stopped and searched the canopy above me. *There!* I squinted hard. *Is that a bird?* "Big bird," I said aloud, trying to break the silence that was pressing down on me.

All movement stopped.

Shit, I thought, holding my breath.

The bird dropped down in front of me. I couldn't take my eyes off the creature as it landed, unfurled its inky wings, and stood to its full height. Blonde hair hung in matted tangles down its back, between its wings, and when my hunter turned to face me, I could see that this creature was a woman with enormous pupils ringed in jade green. She smiled savagely and started toward me. Her movements were jerky, as though she wasn't used to walking.

Run, my brain screamed, but my feet wouldn't comply.

The raven-woman closed the distance between us, grabbed a handful of my hair, and inhaled deeply. "Where. Is. She?"

I was shaking. "Where is who? I don't know anyone! I don't even know where I am!"

She threw my hair in my face. "Zeus almighty!" Then her eyes narrowed. "No matter. I'll find her later."

She leapt into the air, and as I released the air from my lungs in relief, I was yanked off the ground. Claws dug into my armpits so tightly that I could feel blood running down my arms. I kicked my legs and raked my nails down the birdlike legs.

The bird-woman smiled down at me as we soared through the clear air and said, "Keep fighting. Your sweat is a seasoning for my coming feast."

On the Edge

An Interlude

Nova trudged slowly back to the Jeep. No keys. No Marissa. No John. They were devastated. *At least Ryan remembered Marissa*, Nova thought. They stepped out of the brush where the Jeep was parked and, for a moment, watched Ryan pace.

He stopped when he saw them. "Well? Where is she?"

"Gone," Nova said simply.

Ryan's face crumpled. "What have I done?"

Nova shrugged; they wanted to be there for Ryan, the way he always had been for them since they were nine. But, dammit, this trip *had* been his idea. Ryan promised they'd be safe because he camped out here all the time. Nova was angry at him.

"Nova? Are you listening to me? I'm going to get her."

Nova snapped out of their angry thoughts. "What? No. Dude, she is gone. Like dead and gone. Those monsters in there…"

Ryan shook his head. "She was my responsibility. You both were."

"And John?"

"What?"

"John is gone too."

Ryan ran a hand through his hair. "We've been over this. I have no idea who John is, but if you say he was here too, then he was also my responsibility. But I do remember Marissa. I have to try."

Nova crossed their arms over their chest. "Then you're going alone."

Ryan nodded resolutely. "I know." He walked past Nova and said, "I'm sorry."

Nova kicked the wheel of the Jeep in frustration, gave Ryan's back the finger, and started slogging in the direction they believed the highway to be.

PART THREE

THE EMPATH

The world is a symphony of color
All contained within the soul.
The oldest of souls are conductors
of the rainbow,
Bringing forth the vibrancy of life
And the muted tones of death.

Ryan

I slogged back into the woods. *So stupid*, I thought, *what was I thinking not using any magic? Gus sold those simple directional spells for a reason. Hell, I keep my own for the same reason!* I tightened my hands into fists and kicked a rock. As I watched it roll off the trail, I felt water hit my head. I glared up at the sky. "Now, it's going to rain?!" I shouted.

But no.

The sky was a perfect, idyllic blue. I wiped the moisture from my hair, and my hand came back bloody. What was happening? I kept scanning the sky, and then I saw it. The biggest eagle I had ever seen. And it had prey in its claws.

I squinted; that was no eagle. "Ris!" I called and took off running in the direction they had flown. I didn't take my eyes off the sky. I had to catch her. I couldn't let anything happen to her.

I ran through stitches in my sides and blazing fires in my lungs. My legs were jelly, and still I kept moving. I couldn't see Ris and her captor anymore, but whatever had caught her was shrieking. I thought my eardrums would explode at the sound.

I was blind to everything around me except what I could see through the canopy of trees. So blind that I didn't stop running until I was stopped by Aggie running full force straight into me. We fell back, and a dust cloud puffed up around us. Coughing, I stood and offered my hand to help her up.

Aggie brushed off her pants and glared at me. "Get out of my way!"

"Aggie! It's Ryan! You have to help me! Something has Marissa!"

"I know! It's why I have to go!"

"No. Please! You have to help us!"

"Us? Who's us?"

"Me, dammit. Help me!"

Aggie smiled cruelly and looked around for Nova. "So you are alone now?"

I swallowed hard. "Yes, but so is Marissa, and I'm going to find her." Aggie laughed, and I realized that Nova had been right from the beginning. I should have fought harder to stay on their side.

"What makes you think you can get to her now?"

"I have to try. There is something out there hunting my friends, and I am going to stop it."

"Such strong words from such a quiet child." Aggie was circling me now. "You, who are alone, think you can stop anything?"

I held my ground. "Who are you?"

She stopped circling and smiled toothily. "The last thing you'll remember."

1750

The musician ran his slender, calloused fingers down the neck of the lute, while his other hand supported the teardrop-shaped base, the wood smooth and cool to the touch. William knew that he had to have this instrument; his current lute had just about been played to death, the wood under the strings worn down so far it was almost impossible for William to form the chords. Unfortunately, this level of perfection would have to wait until he made some money from this town.

"She's a real beauty, isn't she?"

William nodded, wavering slightly on his feet when he felt the floor tilt.

"I just finished her today, but the customer I made her for changed his mind." Ben eyed the potential sale in front of him. "I don't suppose you'd be interested in a lute, would you?"

William sighed, and the proprietor rocked back on his heels as his nostrils were assaulted by the fumes of rancid mead. "I'm sorry to say that as of right now my billfold is a bit thin." William continued to eye the lute in his hands, from the fresh new strings to the deep-red rose that adorned the face. "But..."

Ben ran a finger discreetly under his nose and looked closer at the intoxicated man before him. Thick, tousled blond hair framed a face that had aged before its time. His clothes were worn and shabbily patched. A small, limp change purse hung from his waist. In that moment, Ben made a decision.

"Well, I'm afraid that I'm going to have to ask you to leave. I welcome those that just want to admire my instruments, but I don't have the space to warm drunken vagrants."

William's head spun around. "Sir, I am not a *vagrant*. I"—he put a hand over his heart and lifted his chin haughtily—"am a traveling troubadour."

Ben gently took the lute from the drunk and set it back on its stand. "Oh. Well, Mr. Troubadour, if you don't have a way to pay for my wares, you need to move on."

William felt himself flush with embarrassment at how he had spent the last of his hard-earned money at the tavern. Just as his father had always done, leaving William and his brother hungry and often alone. No, he was not his father.

William was successful at his trade. Westley had made sure of that, teaching him how to entertain people while he played. Westley loved music—it was his whole heart—but he didn't have William's talent. Westley had known that William would be a great musician. In that, and that alone, he hadn't let Westley down.

The embarrassment turned quickly to anger. Who was this man to judge him? To turn him away because he had one drink too many? William clenched his fists as he fought to keep himself on even ground. "You listen to me, *sir*," he sneered. "I might not have the money right now to purchase anything, but that does not mean you should speak to me this way."

Ben had been steering William toward the door during his speech, and once William was outside, Ben shoved him and smartly shut the door, leaving William standing in the dusty road.

*

The woodsy scent fills my nostrils,
Quickly followed by bile.
On the first whiff, I close my eyes
And understand the draw to
That amber liquid.

*

William sat at a table in a dark corner of the saloon. Fuming, his mind kept circling back to the same thoughts. *Who does that man think he is? So what if I stopped here on my way to the music shop? If that damned shop owner had let me say anything further before shoving me out the door, he would have found out that I will have money after my show tonight.* He smiled with dark pride. Most traveling musicians made a pittance at their shows, but William had a gift; he could play people out of their next month's rent.

"Hey, aren't you that minstrel fellow?"

William lifted his head and narrowed his eyes at the barkeep. "Excuse me? I am not a *minstrel*. I am a *troubadour*."

The tavern owner nodded. "Well, whoever you are, aren't you supposed to be out there?"

William stood so quickly that his chair fell behind him. "Dammit!" He ran for the door shouting, "Put those drinks on my tab!"

*

The liquid courage seeps from
His pores.
The misplaced confidence masks
His stumbling steps.
His life is performance.

*

It was almost full dark by the time William reached his performance area. He looked at the small field before him. Red and yellow flags marked the entrance to the performance grounds; torches illuminated the perimeter and lined the center aisle. Within the circle of torches were simple wooden benches that the townspeople occupied. Most sat facing forward, waiting patiently for the show to start, but there were a handful of people in attendance who were shifting in their seats and looking around.

William wiped the sweat from his brow and focused on walking the straight path down the center aisle. He reached the small stage, which he had set up that morning, turned to face the audience, and realized— *My lute.* In his rush, he had left it at the tavern. He huffed, irritated; that tavern owner had probably kept it as payment. *Well, now what?*

He smiled hesitantly at the crowd. "Good evening, everyone." William pitched his voice so that even the people in the back could hear him. "I know you're all here to have a nice evening of music, but it appears I've lost my lute."

The whole crowd groaned, except for one blonde woman who sat front and center. Unlike the rest of the people in attendance, whose clothes were plain and unadorned—the men in simple tunics and work britches; the women, heavy wool dresses with linen shifts, their hair covered in snoods— this beautiful woman wore a rich-violet dress and pale-green shift. The color choice made her green eyes take on an unearthly glow. Her hair flowed loose and was uncovered as it curled down her back.

William locked eyes with her and was immediately at sea. She smiled as William continued to stand completely dumb-struck. After what could have been several minutes or just a few seconds, William came to himself. "I'm sorry to tell you that, without my lute, I'm afraid I won't be able to perform."

The crowd, including the woman in the front row, surged angrily to their feet. But instead of yelling with the rest of them, the woman simply held up a hand and silenced the crowd. "Now, I'm sure that you can perform without your lute. Can't you keep rhythm?"

William gaped at the audacity of this woman. *Is no one going to stop her from speaking out of turn? Does beauty really buy that kind of power?*

"Uh, I am a musician. Of course, I can keep rhythm, but I'm afraid I don't have any drums."

The woman laughed musically, and the crowd joined her. "You have hands, don't you?"

William nodded, looking down at hands that no longer seemed to belong to him. The whole situation had been wrenched from his control, and William felt incapable of getting it back.

"Well, good. I'll start you off, and so long as you clap along with me, I think we can put a show together." She was laughing at him, and there was nothing he hated more than being made a fool. Still, there was nothing for it. Maybe he would share the evening's take with her. *Maybe.*

The woman turned to face the crowd, and in a voice that sounded much more confident than William felt the woman should be, she shouted, "Good evening, my good people! My name is Agatha, and *we* are going to put on a show for you!" Agatha pushed her hair over her shoulders and turned to face William. She started clapping.

Against his better judgment, he joined in, clapping quietly at first. But as soon as Agatha started to sing, William began to clap in earnest.

The first song she sang was a jaunty tune that at the time was popular amongst traveling musicians. The people sang along. They were so enthusiastic about the music that some people even started dancing around the benches. Agatha then slowed her clapping, and William followed suit; her next song was a ballad that he had never heard before. He turned to the audience and watched with awe as the people who had just been dancing sat on their benches and clasped hands. Couples leaned their heads together and closed their eyes dreamily as she sang hauntingly.

What magic is this?

Agatha turned to William, and he thought her smile hardened slightly as they continued to perform together. William brushed it off and continued to follow her rhythm as she sang her way through an entire repertoire of songs. Some he knew; most he didn't. William smiled to himself. *I'll have to find a way to convince her to share her music with me.*

Just as he finished that thought, Agatha stopped singing and thanked everyone for coming out. William held his hat out and waited for people to come forward with their money, as they always did; tonight, though, the crowd stood and shuffled toward home.

William whirled on his impromptu partner. "What just happened? Why did they leave without paying us?"

Agatha shrugged. "It's not always about the money. Tonight, it was about giving the people something to remember."

"All right, but I need to eat."

"And drink," Agatha said under her breath.

"Now you listen here—"

"No, *you* listen here. Something wonderful happened here tonight, and people will be talking about it for weeks and months to come. And it happened because I saved you. I didn't have to, but like you said, we've got to eat."

William stared agog at her. "But we didn't eat. Anything. How are we going to eat?"

Agatha crossed her arms over her chest. "Well, it's late, so you're not going to be able to find any supper tonight, but I'll pay for your breakfast in the morning."

"How are we going to pay for it?"

Agatha sighed heavily and dropped her arms to her sides. "Come on. I'll walk with you to the inn."

She stormed off, leaving William confused as to what just happened. After making no money today, how did she expect them to eat tomorrow? *We'll perform tomorrow, and I'll make sure the people pay then,* he thought. William was exhausted, but he had no choice but to follow Agatha. He struggled to keep up as her long strides ate up the ground they covered.

They arrived at the inn, and just as William was about to say his "Good night," Agatha strode into the inn and walked up to what he realized must be her room. Just his luck, she was also traveling. Then he realized that she must be traveling alone; a woman on the road alone was vulnerable.

William's luck really was changing.

*

In the depth of night
The mask comes off.
Reality seeps in.
Plumes of old hurts and old angers surface.
The need for the cure tightens its grasp.

*

William blinked dryly into the sunlight streaming through his window. He groaned and turned his face into the pillow. This was turning into a disaster. No money, no lute, no plan. *Well,* he thought, *not a whole plan.* He rolled onto his back and scrubbed his face with his hands. Agatha was his new meal ticket, but to get that ticket, he had to get up.

William saw Agatha as he came downstairs, and he was struck by how stony her face was. Had he imagined all the warmth from the night before? He watched her as she was looking out the window. She was absently scratching at her arm, and something was poking through one of the sleeves. He watched as Agatha pulled at the thing and slowly removed a dove-grey feather from her sleeve. She glared at it before throwing it to the ground.

Before William could process what he had just seen, Agatha turned and smiled brilliantly. "Good day! I was just about to call for the guard to check on you!"

William walked over and met Agatha at the window. "I apologize for my tardiness. I'm afraid our performance last night did me in."

"Yes, I'm sure that's all it was."

William ignored the snide remark. "Shall we go to breakfast?"

"I'm afraid that it's a bit late for breakfast now. But I will take you to lunch." Without waiting, Agatha strode out of the inn and into the blazing light of the early afternoon. She stopped in front of the tavern where William had unwittingly paid for his liquid meals with his lute. "So do they have actual food here or just drink?"

William shrugged, and it occurred to him that he hadn't actually eaten anything since he had arrived in town the day before. No wonder he felt so off-kilter. "I hope they have food, but I still don't—"

Agatha held up a hand to cut him off as she walked straight into the tavern. "Ladies and gentlemen, your afternoon entertainment has arrived!"

William's mouth fell open as he heard the proclamation. He walked forward, braced his hands on the door, and swallowed a mouthful of bile before straightening his clothes and smoothing his hair back, away from his face. He was all smiles when he walked into the tavern that the night before had been romantically lit by candles on every table; now, it looked dingy and small in the glaring daylight streaming through the windows.

Agatha turned to look at him; her face lit up into a smile. "Allow me to introduce my companion, William. Now, please forgive us as this partnership is fairly new; we are still getting to know each other. William, love, do play any instrument instead of clapping your hands?"

The crowd laughed, and William felt nothing but humiliation. Who did she think she was? He was the talent; Agatha was just a woman. William continued to smile as he joined her in the center of the tables. "Well, darling, I happen to play the lute, but it appears I have misplaced it somewhere in our travels."

Aggie nodded and spun with a flourish to the man at the bar. "Good sir, is that a lute I see behind your bar?"

The oily man picked up the lute roughly by the neck and held it aloft, all the while looking William square in the eyes. "You mean this one? I suppose I could let you all borrow it. So long as you promise to return it. It has…sentimental value to me."

Agatha must not have noticed the animosity between William and man behind the bar because she nodded sagely before taking the lute and handing it to William. "I assure you, sir, it will be returned as soon as we are finished. Now, for our terms. We would love to play for you and your guests, but I'm afraid we will need lunch when we are finished."

The tavern owner leaned on the bar and licked his lips. "Let's hear a song first; then we'll talk."

Agatha smiled brightly and turned to the people enjoying their meals. "Did you all hear that? We get to perform for you!"

The diners cheered.

Agatha gestured William into a chair, and she took her place at his shoulder. She inhaled deeply and began to sing. Just as the night before, the crowd was immediately enraptured, only this time William found himself losing focus. He kept shaking his head to clear the fog, but it was relentless. The more William tried to clear it, the thicker it rolled in …until there was nothing but grey. And singing.

As William felt himself dissolving into the fog, he continued to hear Agatha's singing. Pieces of him were being yanked away with each note. There was almost nothing left when, all of a sudden, the singing stopped, the fog evaporated, and William's vision cleared to see Agatha bent at the waist and vomiting all over the floor. William pushed himself out of the way, disgusted.

Agatha's heaves finally subsided, and she lowered herself into a chair. As she caught her breath, she covered her face with her hands. "What is that? Why do I feel like this?"

William approached the table cautiously, sat down, and said, "Well, this is what happens when you sing for the *music* and not the *money*. You get sick. Barman!" William turned to the bar. "Bring us the soup of the day, along with bread…and wine." William looked at the man behind the bar, who hadn't responded; it didn't appear as though he could see or hear anything. William stood and snapped his fingers loudly in the air. "Sir! We need some food and drink over here!"

Suddenly the barkeep came to and started spooning out the soup. "You definitely earned it. I am sorry that your companion was so ill. Suzy! There is a mess out here that needs cleaning."

William looked around; everything was happening in slow motion. It was as though everyone had fallen asleep at once, and they were all slowly coming around at the same time. He sat back in his chair and just watched the world slowly come back to life around him. Agatha's breath shuddered, and William turned his attention to her. "We've got some soup coming. It should help."

Agatha laughed quietly, knowing that wasn't true. "William, I don't know how you perform when you feel like this."

"Sometimes it's the only way I can perform," William said, realizing that he felt better than he had in days.

"Why would you do this to yourself night after night, and apparently day after day?"

William thought for a moment and then shook his head. "You know, I don't know anymore. I feel as though I had a reason, but now it's gone."

The tavern owner set their meals down in front of them. William reached for only the bread and wine, while Agatha sniffed apprehensively at the soup. "You should eat something," the man said before going back to the bar.

Agatha nodded, poked at the soup with her spoon, and toyed with a piece of bread, but still ate nothing. William watched Agatha and shrugged before shoving a heel of bread in his mouth, washing it down with wine. They sat in the tavern together for hours—bouts of conversation followed by companionable silences that William filled with more wine. Agatha seemed to know exactly how to draw William out in conversation, and the free-flowing wine helped smooth the way.

William even found himself telling Agatha about the lute from the day before. The dream lute that was polished to a shine, the one that had a deep-red rose painted on its face and thorny vines that wound around the sound hole. She commiserated with him over the poor treatment from the shop owner, and even helped him hatch a plan to steal the lute as she poured him a final glass of wine.

Full of food and wine, William leaned back in his chair, and his lips curved into a sardonic smile. "Yes, let's go get my lute."

*

Courage, hubris, and numbness
All wash out of the tumbler and into the brain.
Arm in arm, we stumble into the night.
To get our just desserts.

*

They waited until the town had fallen quiet. William linked arms with his beautiful companion, and together they staggered through the streets toward William's goal. They giggled loudly as they tripped over each other's feet. "Shhh!"

Agatha held a long, slender finger to her lips, while she supported William with her other arm.

William cleared his throat and tried to quiet his laughter. He glanced over at Agatha and was almost sorry that he was going to take her songs and leave her high and dry. He thought about how much money he would make singing those songs about love, and heartache, and soaring over the sea. That music that had rendered two audiences—and who knows how many before that—completely dumbstruck.

And for what? For the love of the *music*? You can't live on the love of the music. Hadn't he learned that the hard way from…*whom?* From whom had he learned that painful lesson? He shook his head, believing that he had had too much to drink. Again.

One foot in front of the other. That's what William needed to focus on. They needed clear thinking if they were going to steal this instrument. He tripped again as Agatha pulled him forward. "Whoa. Slow down." William felt his eyes float in their sockets.

Agatha giggled, but there was something about the sound that didn't ring true. "Oops. Sorry, I'm just so excited to see your new lute. Think of all the beautiful music we'll be making together."

"Maybe we could stop for just a minute." William pulled his arm free and bent at the waist. He felt muddled and confused. He knew he had to have the lute, but he didn't know why anymore. He tried to think back to their lunch, and all he could remember was some bread and so much wine. William straightened and studied Agatha, who was watching him impatiently. Didn't she drink with him? Of course, she did; they were celebrating their new partnership.

All right. New plan. They would get the lute…and then they would head out of town…and then he would get her music. He'd always had an ear for music; all she would have to do is sing for him once or twice, and the songs would be his. He narrowed his eyes, he would have to do this without wine, because he'd be damned if he could remember the songs that she had sung that day.

They arrived in front of the music store and stood facing the door. Agatha picked up a stone that lined the short walk up to the entrance. "Well, no time like the present." She handed the stone to William. "Let's get what's coming to you."

The glass shattered as the stone went through the window. The noise was louder than William had thought it would be; everything was always louder at night. He looked around wildly as Agatha shoved him forward.

"Well? Go on. Let's get it and get out of here."

William finished knocking glass out of the window and climbed through the opening, into the dark store. There it was. His lute. He lifted it off the stand and stood admiring it.

Agatha shouted, "Quick, someone heard us!"

William threw the lute over his shoulder and climbed back out of the window, but in his haste, he cut his hand. "Dammit."

"Come on! We've got to go!" Agatha grabbed William's injured hand and pulled him into the street. "Run!"

William took off, leaving Agatha behind. As he reached the edge of the town's main street, he heard her singing. He stopped and turned. It was too dark to see anything, but her voice floated to him on the air...and once again the fog rolled in.

*

In the end, we all come to the same place.
We all have to answer for living choices.
Will you make excuses, or
Will you own them?

*

When William came to, he was walking through the forest with Agatha by his side. He had the lute, and his hand had been bandaged. "Where are we?"

"Away from the angry townspeople who were looking for you."

William nodded. "What happened to my hand?"

"You had a clumsy getaway."

He tried to make a fist. The pain was excruciating. "How am I supposed to play my songs now?"

Agatha shrugged. "It'll heal."

"That's awfully cold for someone who just convinced me to commit a robbery and then ran away with me."

Agatha stopped and turned to William, her green eyes flashing. "Listen. The only reason we are still *together*," she sneered, "is because of your drinking." She continued under her breath, "It's the only thing I can figure out; you don't have that strong a disposition."

"What the hell is that supposed to mean?"

"Oh, please, like you're really planning on taking me with you from now until forever? You think I don't know that you want my songs?"

William crossed his arms over his chest. "Oh, like you were so successful before me? You don't even sing for money."

Agatha drew her hair over one shoulder and planted her hands on her hips. "I don't need money to be successful. My survival is my success."

"Without money? How can you even do that?"

"I sing. God, you're thick."

William ignored the insult and pushed ahead. "Which is beautiful, but I plan to make your songs more beautiful by adding my voice and my lute."

Agatha was incredulous. "You what? You think you can do what I do? You're human!"

"What does that have to do with anything? So are you!"

Agatha's lips curved into a toothy grin, and for the first time, William saw her fangs. "Oh, I am, am I?"

William started to back up. "Obviously, we have misunderstood each other. You know, we can still be partners. Travel together. I mean, you have to admit your songs sound much better with my accompaniment. Why don't we join up? You can sing for the love of the music, and I'll perform for the money."

"So that you can steal my songs? And then what? Kill me?"

"No. Obviously, I wouldn't kill you. Couldn't kill you." William put his hands up in a gesture of surrender.

Agatha stood still and considered the simpering man before her. "Let's say we do travel together. What's to keep you from taking off on me? Because you have a point—the lute did add something to the music. And I don't know how to play an instrument as fine as that."

William took a cautious step forward. "That's right. This lute is very fine, and we are a great team."

Agatha's arm snaked out, and she grabbed William. "No. I'm sorry. I've seen enough of your life to know that this won't play out the way you're telling me. I know you can't remember this now, but I saw how you turned your back on your brother after he spent his whole life teaching you to play, teaching you to love music. But all you cared about was the money. Just. Like. Your. Father." She punctuated each word with a finger jab to his chest.

William's mouth fell open. "What are you talking about?" He searched his mind, and all he found were holes. There was no memory of a brother, only some of wondering if they were going to have enough money for food. There was no memory of learning to love music, only some of knowing that he wouldn't go hungry so long as he kept playing.

"You left him. Your brother gave you everything, and you left him. Alone. In that hovel. For money. I know you will do the same to me." Agatha started to hum.

"No, stop." The fog rolled in quickly this time, but before he lost all sense of reality, William jumped on top of Agatha and closed his hands around her throat. "I don't know what magic you have, but you will not take what I have left."

Agatha kicked and fought at William. He held her tighter. She started clawing his hands. His livelihood was destroyed in seconds after her talons came out. William shrieked and fell off her. He lay on the ground, looking at his shredded hands. He would never play again; everything he had worked for was gone.

Agatha coughed and rubbed her neck as she sat up. She crawled to where William lay sobbing, pulled her skirts up, and straddled William. "It's time to finish this." William's tear-filled eyes glazed over as Agatha sang to him.

She continued to sing as she slid her hooked talon across his throat.

She continued to sing as she watched William bleed out.

When it was over, she stood and shook her skirts out. She looked down the road; she was still miles away from the next town. Word had probably reached them that William was coming. How would she explain this?

Well, she thought, *I am, for all intents and purposes, a woman. Alone. It would make sense if I came screaming into town.* She nodded, satisfied with her plan.

Aggie plaited her hair and lifted the lute from where William had dropped it. "It is really a very nice lute." She slid the strap across her shoulders and strummed a few of the chords she had just learned. "Yes, that will add a very nice touch to my songs." She pushed the lute to her back and nestled it between what was left of her wings.

Agatha took off running and started to shriek.

Ryan

"Hi," I said, but the kid in front of me didn't answer. I tried again. "Hi." Nothing. "Hello?" Finally, the kid looked at me from the swing they were on. I knew they were cool because their color was a beautiful swirly white. I had never seen it before, and it reminded me of what I thought a ghost would look like. "Can I swing next to you?"

They looked around. "Are you talking to me?"

I laughed; this was all playing out exactly as I remembered it. "Yes. Why wouldn't I be?" At the time, I had been so confused by this response.

They swirled a red tennis shoe through the wood chips. "No one ever wants to play with me. No one ever even talks to me. Not even the teachers."

I felt my heart break again. When I'd heard this at eight, it had crushed me. But now, understanding what was actually happening, it was worse. I sat down in the swing; at the time, there had been so much space in it, but now I was adult-sized and not made for playground swings.

I smiled and said, "Well, I'm talking to you."

Eight-year-old Nova looked over at me and choked out, "You won't forget me, will you?"

I frowned at Nova. "What do you mean?"

Nova looked down, but it didn't hide their tears. "When people do actually talk to me, they never remember me. Or even see me again."

I pushed myself gently back and forth. "I hope I'll be able to see you again. I'll do my best."

*

I woke up rubbing my head. I looked over at Aggie. She was sobbing, but I felt zero sympathy. "What the hell? Now we're never going to get to Marissa!"

Aggie rubbed her sleeve across her face. "Too much. You're too much." She looked over at me, her face shiny and red. "You just walk around like this?"

"Like what?" My head hurt, but the dizziness had subsided.

Aggie gestured at her splotchy face and shuddered out another breath. "Like this. All this…this…"

"Empathy?" I asked, slowly getting to my feet.

"YES! This is so painful!"

I laughed, annoyed. "You get used to it." Aggie took some deep breaths while I debated my next move. "I'm sure running will do me no good, right?"

"Well. At this point, it's either me or *her*."

I thought about what had been happening so far on this trip, and all of those missing hikers. "Actually, it's probably both of you, or just her."

Aggie looked confused. "Are you giving up?"

I shrugged. "From what I'm gathering, once you had us, we didn't stand a chance."

Aggie sighed and pressed the heels of her hands to her eyes. "In your defense, I really had no idea what I was getting into when I summoned you four into my circle in the first place."

Now, I was confused. "What do you mean four?"

She gestured vaguely with one hand. "You know your little troupe had a lot of power in it. I could have just stopped at your friend. But you were all just too delicious."

I squinted at her. "Marissa didn't have any power."

Aggie sneered, "Not her. The other one. The StoryKeeper. John."

I shook my head, both in denial and at the holes in my memories. "I have no idea who you're talking about."

"Of course, you don't. Come on; let's get moving."

"Why? Why not just take care of me here?"

"Because I'm full, and if we don't keep moving, she'll find me." Aggie walked over and kicked my pack.

"Fine," I said.

"You know, you remind me of my husband."

I started. "You? You were married?"

Aggie nodded. "I had to blend in, especially back then. People then were not as kind as they are now to single women traveling alone."

I looked at her closely. Her words didn't match her tone, and since she didn't have an aura to speak of, I had to rely on good old-fashioned observations. "Well, since it looks like we're going to be walking for a while, why don't you tell me about him?"

Aggie shifted her pack and lute. "How's your history?"

"As good as the next English major's. Why?"

"My husband was the first fatality of the Hartford Witch Trials."

I stopped short. "How old are you?"

"Old enough, now keep moving. The trees are hurting my eyes."

I started walking again. "Fine. At least explain to me what is happening here."

Aggie didn't answer. I could hear her walking behind me; her thoughts were streaming off her in waves. *How did I miss this before? Her mind never stops.* I looked around and rubbed my forehead; the forest colors were duller than I remembered. "Must be my head injury," I muttered. I chanced a look back at Aggie; curled around her throat were ribbons of acidic yellow.

"What are you looking at?" Aggie demanded.

"Nothing. Just wondering how your throat is feeling."

"I'm fine. I just want to get out of here," she said through clenched teeth.

"Me too." My voice cracked. As angry as I was at Nova and this whole situation, I was more terrified. I knew I wasn't going to make it out of here, but maybe I could find a way to get a message out there. To Gus, maybe, or my family.

Aggie inhaled deeply. "Oh, good. I didn't think I'd get grief."

I spun around. "Enough! That is enough!"

Aggie laughed cruelly. "You've got some bite to you too."

"Only for special occasions." I turned and kicked something. Keys.

Aggie shoved past me and picked up the familiar key ring. "Finally. Let's make tracks. Do you think Nova is still waiting for you at the Jeep?" I felt the color drain from my face. "I'm not gonna lie; I've been saving them for last. I've never encountered that type of magic before. What say, Ryan, should we go check?" She narrowed her eyes and spun the keys around on a finger.

Something snapped. I couldn't save Marissa or myself. But I could give Nova a fighting chance. I dropped my pack and took off. My legs pumped, and my lungs were on fire within seconds. I should have worked out more. Just like... I stumbled when I couldn't remember who used to invite me to exercise. I tripped again, and this time I landed on my forearms and knees.

"Get up!" I screamed as music filled my ears. I stood and took off again. I hoped I was going in the right direction, away from the highway, farther into the Pacific Crest. My only focus now was getting as far from Nova as possible. I could still save them.

Aggie's voice surrounded me. I stopped running and spun around. "You coward!" I shouted at the sky. "You can't even face me yourself!" The grey was pressing down on me. I closed my eyes and started meditating.

Breathe in.

"I can hear the wind." *Lies, all I can hear is Aggie's singing.*

Breathe out.

"I can smell the earth."

Breathe in.

I opened my eyes. "I can see the colors of life." Except, I couldn't. I was surrounded on all sides by mist. I forced myself to unclench my fists and keep breathing.

Breathe out.

"I am the wind."

Breathe in.

"I am the Earth."

Breathe out.

"I am life."

A hand closed around my throat. "You're mine."

1648

Murmurs float on the air.
"Witchcraft."
Hands tied, because
To deny is to
Lie.
To admit truth is to
Die.

*

Agatha's eyes opened to the incessant shouting of the town crier. She groaned and rolled over, burying her face in her arms. As if she hadn't known what today was. As if it weren't all the town had been talking about since the trial.

Today was Execution Day.

The crier's voice faded as he screamed his way back toward town. His next stop was going to be the inn, where he would nail up all the lurid details of her husband's coming demise. Agatha smiled tightly. It was time to face the coming day. She sat up and stretched her arms above her head. Her scarred shoulder blades pulled tight across her back.

She winced, slightly aggravated. "It's been centuries, and still it hurts." Pushing to her feet, she contemplated her wardrobe choices. "Should I go with the black dress? Or the black dress?" Goddess, Agatha hated Puritans.

Agatha braided her hair and tightly wound it into a bun at the base of her neck, before covering her head with the scratchy linen cap. It was the start of the summer heat, and she still had to wear wool tights and a heavy wool dress.

She sighed and made her way to the door. She took her hat off the rack and, with a final rallying sigh, stepped out into the sun. Agatha strode forward, her steps quick and sure, as the wool of her skirts dragged around her ankles. She slid a finger into the collar of her dress to try to loosen it.

As she neared the town, Agatha stopped and watched the people milling around. "Mortals," she muttered under her breath, and in a public show of vanity, she adjusted the hat that was precariously balanced on the linen cap. Agatha could already feel the pressure of the townspeople's judgment. She lowered her head and started forward again, this time with purposeful hesitation. Hands folded piously, head bowed so low she felt her neck might snap, Agatha hummed lightly under her breath. She delighted in the woody, weighty taste of everyone's distaste and judgment. What hypocrites they all were, the people of Hartford.

When John was first arrested, the townspeople turned on her, again. She offered to save John, but he refused. He told her he was done running. Done hiding. Agatha was devastated, but in the end, she relented. Better to save herself than to carry around human baggage.

Not that John was baggage. Exactly. *And yet...* Agatha shook her head. No, he had been very clear on the whole situation from the very beginning, in fact. Agatha smiled at the memory.

*

She was lying in wait for a meal when a man rode by. From her hiding place in the grass, Agatha—*No, not Agatha, not yet; I was still Aglaope then*—began to sing. But her voice hit a wall, so she sang louder.

The rider pulled up on the reins, and his horse wheeled around. He scanned the road. "Come out. Whatever you are. Show yourself."

Aglaope pressed herself into the grass, trying to make herself invisible.

"It's no use. I know something is out there. I can feel you, even though you are trying to use your power." He dismounted and walked his horse back down the road toward her.

Aglaope took a chance and started to sing one more time. The music hit the invisible wall around the man and lit up with blue electricity.

He let go of his horse's reins and took one more step forward. He looked around again, and his black eyes met hers. "Gotcha."

Aglaope was mortified. She stood up and tried to take off toward the forest. She heard the man say a string of words, after which she was yanked off her feet and dragged backward to him. Aglaope was spun around, her toes barely touching the ground.

"Hello there."

"Good day," Aglaope rasped against the invisible hand that held her throat.

"Is there some reason that you were using magic?"

Aglaope struggled. "Is there a reason you are right now?"

"Fair play, you impudent witch."

"I am not a witch."

"Well, you aren't human."

"Maybe you should set me down."

The man narrowed his eyes at Aglaope. "If I do, you can't run. Give me your word."

"You have it. I won't run." After the stranger let Aglaope down, she rubbed her neck and took several deep breaths. "You sure pack a punch."

"I'm sure you do as well."

"Don't patronize me."

"I'm not. If not for my wards, I'm sure you would have been able to kill me, or whatever it was you were trying to do."

"I don't kill people. Not anymore."

The man laughed gruffly. "I'm John."

"I'm Agla…" She hesitated. She had just recently learned the power of true names and was not ever going to offer hers again. *Agatha. I'm Agatha now.* "I'm Agatha."

"I don't think I caught that. Did you say Agatha?"

"Yes, I'm sorry. You were really holding me tight; I was struggling to say my name."

"I apologize about that. Can I take you somewhere?"

"Sir, what would people think? We are in Puritan country."

John thought for a moment. "Well, it seems we are at an impasse. I can't have you going into the next town and telling everyone about the witch you met."

Agatha agreed. "And I can't have you doing the same, even though I am *not* a witch." Agatha ran her hands through the tangles in her hair.

"Well, I'm headed to Hartford. I was unceremoniously excommunicated from my last village. I'm hoping that I'm far enough away to keep word from reaching here. We could go to Hartford together."

"Excuse me? I have already said why that would be insane."

"Not if we were married."

"What?"

"Convenience. Purely out of convenience. What better way to keep each other's secrets? We'll keep each other in line. I don't see what other option we have."

*

> No one is safe from
> The burning stares,
> Silent accusations.

Who will be next?

Him? Me?

Time to make a choice.

*

A lot has changed in the past three years, Agatha thought as she paused in front of the inn to read the decree the town crier posted.

By Order of the Towne of Hartford

On the day of our Lord, June 1, 1648,

Goodman John Audley

has been found

Guilty of witchcraft

and, as such, has been named a Heretic.

Goodman John Audley is hereby

Sentenced to Death

by

Pressing under the weight of his sins

made earthly by stones.

Sentenced to be carried out on June 21, 1648.

Agatha's eyes filled with sudden and unexpected grief. She had been living in the world of men for too long. Emotions were useless things. Tears even more so. Agatha roughly dried the wetness from her cheeks.

"It is a sign of vanity to rosy your cheeks," said a voice from behind her.

Agatha frowned and turned. "Goody Basset. How are you today?"

Goody Basset held up her Bible. "Just on my way to worship. As you should be too. Who else will pray for Goodman Audley's soul if not his wife?"

"I will worship when the injustice against my husband has been righted."

Goody Basset clutched her collar. "The only injustice is that you were found innocent and are not rotting in prison with your witch husband."

Agatha leaned forward and said quietly, "Be careful who you condemn. You could be next."

Goody Basset paled to a marble grey, and Agatha continued on her outcast's journey.

*

This is only the beginning.
Hysteria travels faster
Than true magic.
I try to keep it at bay,
But my voice is no match
For pure intention.

*

As warm as it was outside, it was an absolute inferno inside the jail. Agatha ran a discreet finger under her nose as she pressed forward.

"So…you've returned," a voice growled from the depths of the cell.

"I promised I would."

"And I told you to stay away."

"You told me a lot of things." Agatha stared through the bars.

John sat in the corner. His hair hung around his face in greasy strings. His face was gaunt with starvation; his eyes fiery with anger. "Why are you here?"

"I am your wife."

"You are nothing."

Agatha pulled her lips back in a mockery of a smile. "I offered to save you."

"More lies. Don't you tire of all the lies?" John leaned forward, and murky light fell across his face, making him look all the more skeletal. "Leave. Now."

Agatha wrapped her hands around the bars. "I gave you my word to stay until the end. It's a shame your end came first."

A shadow fell over Agatha. "It's time."

Agatha bowed her head and retreated from the cell. She watched through lowered lids as the jailer half-dragged a shackled John to the waiting cart. Agatha took her place next to John, but outside the cart, and remembered her own ride through town.

*

The council came in the pink light of predawn. Agatha was still in her dressing gown, drinking her morning tea. John was out working the fields already.

The front door burst open.

"Goody Audley, you are accused."

Grabbing her under each arm, two men, whom John had called friends, threw Agatha into the cart. Agatha demanded to know the charges, her accuser, anything, but fell silent when she saw John waiting at the edge of the field, his black eyes boring into her.

As she rode through the town, the residents threw garbage, shouted slurs. Agatha ignored it. She'd be free by nightfall, and then she and John would flee Hartford. Together. They arrived at the town hall, and Agatha allowed herself to be dragged inside. She was forced to stand before the council, but remained silent while they fired accusations at her.

Finally, when the men had exhausted themselves, Goodman Basset turned his red face to her and blustered, "Well, Goody Audley, what say you to these claims?"

Agatha smiled felinely and began to sing. One by one, the councilmen's faces went slack. When Agatha's voice faded, Goodman Basset looked at Agatha, smiled benignly, and said, "Thank you for your time. You are free to go."

Agatha walked home, still only in her dressing gown, while the townspeople parted and watched her in shock. No one offered her a covering. She walked in the house and found John rocking by the fire. "You didn't try to stop them."

"What?"

"I know you saw. You didn't try to stop them."

"You were found to be a witch. I couldn't be seen with you anymore."

"Well, I've been found innocent. But we need to leave. It's only a matter of time before they come for you."

"We won't be running. You gave your word you wouldn't run."

Agatha stood completely agog. "But it's you. *You* are the witch! I'm trying to protect you!"

"You will do no such thing. You were foolish today, using your powers that way. I knew you couldn't resist, though. It was a test. You failed."

Agatha's face folded into resigned anger. "A test?"

"And you failed," John repeated. "Now, if you'll excuse me, I need to go to bed…and pray."

"John, know this. When they come for you—and they *will* come because, according to them, 'Witches are the only ones who can identify other witches'—I give you my word that I will be here until the end."

John's eyes clouded over with misgiving, and he began to pray.

*

Agatha was pulled from her reverie as the cart came to a stop at the town square. She watched as John was carried to the bench on the platform, his head held high and his eyes alight with pride. He was laid out, his hands and feet chained down.

Agatha held her breath, still expecting him to use his considerable magic to escape. This was the end. There was one final thing that Agatha could do for John. He was without his wards; he would feel everything.

She glued her eyes to John and began to sing, pouring everything she had into him. He went lax, and Agatha struggled to maintain her breath as she felt the weight of the first stone that pressed the air out of John's lungs. Her voice faded, but remained true, as she felt every stone as more weight was piled onto John. The first snap of his ribs, fluid filling his lungs, drowned her voice until it began to break and bubble as though Agatha were the one suffocating.

They took their last breath together, and with one final tear, Agatha turned and walked out of Hartford.

Ryan

I sat with my mom. We were knee to knee, and I could feel
our breathing was in sync. We had done this together every
day since I started elementary school. Other people were so
overwhelming for me that when I started kindergarten, I came
home sobbing. There is so much pain everywhere. And where
there is joy, there is a different kind of pain. Light so blinding it
explodes behind my eyes.

"Breathe in."

"We hear the wind."

"Breathe out."

"We can smell the Earth."

"Breathe in."

"We can see the colors of life."

"Breathe out."

"We are life."

I smiled sadly at my mother. "You have to go, don't you?"

*She nodded, her robin's-egg blue aura fading until I could see
her weatherworn, peachy face.*

I swiped a hand across my wet face. "I'm sorry."

I blinked, and she was gone; in her place was Aggie. She was looking around frantically.

"How am I here? What have you done?"

I shrugged apathetically. "I don't know. Nothing consciously."

Aggie screamed in frustration.

"That's not going to help. The only thing that wakes away the pain is talking about it. That and breathing."

"That is the stupidest thing I have ever heard."

I laughed wetly, still sucking back tears. "I know. I hate it too. But if you're going to be taking my skill, then you should probably learn a little bit about it."

"How did you know?" Aggie's eyes narrowed.

"My ability was fading, and Nova... Anyway, you should come back here and sit with me."

Aggie reluctantly came back and sat facing me. "Why are you helping me?"

"Because the longer you're in here with me, the farther Nova can get from you."

"Well, you're honest. I'll give you that," Aggie grumbled. She folded her legs and allowed her knees to touch mine.

I cringed and then felt unbearably sad. "You weren't always like this." The grey pressed in suddenly and then released as if it were visible speaker feedback. I held up my hands. "Sorry, old habits. Let's get this over with."

I placed my hands on my knees, and Aggie mirrored me. I walked Aggie through the ritual, and for the first time, I spoke my mother's part out loud.

As Aggie's breathing evened out, the heavy mist began to lighten, and I could feel the warmth of the sun. I looked around.

We are on a beach?

Aggie and I continued to breathe together. The vise of bile around Aggie's neck spread until I could see that she was encased in betrayal. "Aggie, look at what you've created here."

She opened her eyes and immediately scrambled back. "How did we get here? I can't be here."

"Where is 'here'?"

"My sisters," *Aggie choked out. She looked at me.* "Please let me leave this place. I can't remember this. I never want to remember this. Them. Ever again."

I shook my head. "I don't have you. It would appear that you have you."

"Why are we here?"

"You tell me. You're the one in control here."

Aggie got up onto her knees. "I'm so empty. All the time. Nothing fills me. I need to forget."

"But you don't, do you? Not really."

Aggie pounded the sand with her fist. "Give me your stories. Give me your magic. Give me your stories! I don't want mine!" *She lunged at me and shrieked into my face.*

*

I woke with a start. Aggie was pressed against a tree, screaming. Her hands were fisted in her hair. I ran to her. "What's wrong? Aggie!"

She shoved me away and turned her back on me. I looked around. Something was very wrong. Everything looked so dull. Had everything always been this lifeless?

"Weird."

Aggie's breath was shuddering in and out, but at least she'd stopped screaming. I looked around again, wondering where Nova was. Then I remembered our fight.

And Marissa. I had to get to Marissa.

Aggie was muttering to herself; something about breathing and colors, but she was still facing away from me. I started backing away…slowly at first, and then I ran. My steps felt heavy and clumsy. I kept tripping on roots and small rocks. I wasn't even sure of the direction I was running in, but if I stopped to consider the alternative… Well, I *couldn't* consider the alternative.

A shriek filled the air. The sound of the same animal that got Marissa. "Shit!"

Then the singing started again, both sounds warring inside my head. "No. No! NO!"

I tripped and landed hard on the ground this time. As I pushed to my feet, I saw it. Midnight wings, giant bird legs, and the body of a woman. She looked hard into my face, her breath heaving.

Aggie's painful singing reached us. The monster looked up, and then she smiled at me. A cruel, terrifying smile. She bent down and picked up a rock. "I'll deal with you later."

Stars exploded in my eyes before darkness closed in.

1610

Beyond the veil
Lies the land of the Fae.
They'll ask for your name.
Beware.
There is power in names.

*

Aglaope was hit with the smell first. Rotting flesh and decay filled her nostrils. Silently pleading for sleep to return, she rolled to her side and covered her nose with her arm. The stench was everywhere. Groaning, Aglaope opened her eyes and was immediately blinded, and the putrid smell was replaced by the pleasant, damp smell of forest.

A curious face was staring at Aglaope. Luminous violet eyes framed by impossibly thick lashes, a pert nose, and a slightly wicked smile. "You're awake."

Aglaope blinked slowly, and when her eyes were partially open, the face in front of her swam and became...*other*. "Yes, I am awake. Perhaps you could back up so that I can sit up. You have me at a disadvantage."

The face backed up, and Aglaope watched the form unfold into a lithe creature with long limbs and gossamer wings colored the same violet as his eyes. "I'm Puck."

Aglaope sat up, and the world tilted. She shook her head before replying. "I'm—"

"Shh." Puck's face contorted with fear. "Don't say it."

"Say what?"

"Puck, my darling Puck, what have you brought for me?"

Puck's wings fluttered as they rose off the ground to turn and face the interloper. "I'm not sure, milady. She appears to have fallen here on her own."

"She?"

Aglaope looked around Puck cautiously and saw an ethereal beauty the likes of which Aphrodite would have found a way to smite. "She. Me. Aglaope."

Puck gasped.

The woman laughed musically; it set Aglaope's teeth on edge. "It is my eternal pleasure to meet you. I am Titania."

*

Take not the offerings of
The Fae.
For you will find yourself
In their debt.
Resist the promises and
Trappings to watch
The glamour crack.

*

The next days passed by in a blur of filmy dresses, music, and languid rest. Aglaope had been traveling for so long she was exhausted and welcomed the rest, which was all this court seemed to do. Aglaope had never encountered such dreamy creatures. The only one who showed any sense of urgency was Puck, who flitted and hovered and did their lady's bidding at a moment's notice.

Aglaope went for a walk one afternoon in the watery sunlight, winding herself through a forest where branches hung low under the weight of the sleepy limbs of Titania's subjects. Along the way, Aglaope became hungry and decided it was time for a simple meal. She began to sing a simple ballad.

She had barely gotten the chorus out when she began to gag on her meal, suffering visions of flesh dripping from the trees, skeletal hands grasping for help, and Puck. Their wings torn to shreds, hanging like rags around their shoulders. Vacant holes where their beautiful eyes used to be. And behind Puck, a dried-out husk of Titania. Gone was the flaming-red hair, and in its place were brittle strands barely attached to the grimy skull. Her flowing dress crumbling and blowing dust everywhere.

Aglaope began to vomit. Puck was by her side in a moment, holding her hair back and rubbing her back. Aglaope stood and looked Puck in their beautiful eyes. "You're not right."

They held a long finger to their lips.

"Aglaope, come and sit with me."

Puck and Aglaope turned; Aglaope's eyes widened with fear.

Puck pushed her forward, whispering, "Don't accept what she offers."

Aglaope climbed onto Titania's bed, which was suspended from two enormous trees with floral vines entwined in them. As Titania ran her fingers up and down Aglaope's arm, she shuddered.

"Are you happy here?"

Aglaope nodded slowly. "I certainly needed the rest."

Titania's hand drifted to a silver bowl that had appeared at her side, and she began to eat purple grapes so ripe they looked as though they could burst at any moment. "Would you like to have a grape?"

Everything around her seemed to hold its breath, as though waiting for her to answer. Aglaope swallowed hard and remembered Puck's warning. "No, thank you." Two sensations flowed through Aglaope—relief and disappointment.

Titania brushed her hands together, as though cleaning off some crumbs. "Well, since you're accepting my hospitality, but not my offerings, perhaps we should discuss your manners."

A sharp crack overhead had Aglaope looking up into a maze of dead branches. She blinked, and they were back to normal. "I don't think I understand."

"You have been welcomed here, and yet you rebuff any offer of mine. It is rude."

Aglaope chose her next words carefully. "It's just that I don't eat...much."

"Yes, well, you must understand. The last guest we had was so rude I turned him into an ass. So there must be something you'll accept from me."

Aglaope choked on nervous laughter. "What?"

Titania nodded and smiled. "Some insufferable writer."

The two fell into an uncomfortable silence. A gentle breeze moved the bed swing, and despite her misgivings, Aglaope was lulled into a drowsy, half-waking state; she lay down. Smiling faintly, Aglaope began to sing.

Immediately, the grassy smell started to melt into that of decaying mildew. Aglaope turned her head and was met with the nightmare vision of Titania lying alongside her. Aglaope's eyes seemed to drift; she took in the sight beyond Titania…and immediately became paralyzed.

Behind Titania was a creature looming over them. Sun-bleached skull with elongated face. Onyx horns swept back in perfect spirals. Body impossibly tall and imposing. Aglaope stopped singing and tried to blink the vision away.

Aglaope watched Titania stretch a dry, bony hand toward the creature that leaned down toward her in response. It was all Aglaope could do not to scream as the two skulls came together in a passionate kiss.

She continued blinking rapidly, and slowly her vision returned to normal. Titania was smiling up at the creature, which was no longer a creature at all, but a magically beautiful man with the horns of a ram growing out of his head.

"Aglaope, please meet King Oberon."

Oberon bowed deeply. "The pleasure is all mine."

*

Fae of the forest play games
With mortals of the Earth.
Fae of the forest hold tightly
Their glamours until
It becomes
Reality.

*

Aglaope leapt up and began to run. She could no longer figure out what was real and what was magic. There was obviously something sinister happening here, but the arrival of the king had been enough. Hands reached down from the trees to grab at Aglaope, and she realized that they weren't lazy creatures of the trees, but that they were bound there by vines of bittersweet.

Aglaope was yanked back by a hand that had managed to grab ahold of her shoulder. She turned and looked into the face of a faerie whose face was frozen in a perpetual scream, yet no sound was audible.

"I need to get out of here. Please help me."

The faerie shook her head and pushed Aglaope away.

She stumbled back into something hard; turning, she saw Puck. Without saying a word, they grabbed her hand and took flight. Wind rushed through Aglaope's hair, and she took a moment to miss the ability to fly. The moment passed, and she held tighter to Puck.

They landed suddenly at a circle of mushrooms. They held both of her shoulders and looked into her eyes. "Beware the circles. Don't come back here." They pushed her, and she fell down through the circle, and in seconds, she was shot up through a circle on the other side.

Gasping for breath, Aglaope looked frantically around; she was standing in the center of the circle of mushrooms. The smell of decay was oozing up through the grass under her feet. Aglaope shrieked and stomped out the circle of mushrooms. The more mushrooms she destroyed, the cleaner the air smelled and the more at peace Aglaope felt. When the last mushroom crumbled under her foot, Aglaope took one last deep breath and started to walk away.

A branch snapped behind her. Aglaope turned and thought she saw a ram disappear into the trees.

RYAN

"*You really won't come with me?*"

I opened my mouth to answer Nova, but someone beat me to it.

"*I don't like any part of this. This journal. You leaving to go find 'the truth.' Besides, I can't just leave school and follow you around to…what? What would I do on this journey?*"

Papers rustled and caused ripples of color behind my eyelids. I kept them closed tight. If I don't open my eyes, she won't get this one. I won't lose this one too. I squeezed my eyes as tight as I could and listened to the conversation escalate around me.

"*Ry, please. I need you.*" *I felt Nova move around me to sit on the floor. They had expected me to get up and sit next to them. But I didn't. This was the moment.*

The moment I lost them.

"*Need me? For what? Nova, maybe you should get some real help, find an outlet for this need to get revenge.*"

"*Not revenge. Justice. Vengeance.*"

Even with my eyes sealed shut, I could see the whole altercation perfectly. I sat at my desk; the only time I took my eyes off my computer screen was to look at Nova's maps and that damn journal. My fists clenched.

That journal was coated in an oily black that stuck to the fingers of everyone who touched it. And slowly it seeped into the person's aura, turning it a muddy version of their own color. I couldn't even look at Nova now. Their aura had always looked as if it had been woven with starlight and dreams. Now, it was dull and gritty, its natural opalescence replaced by gravel so heavy that it was slowing Nova's every move.

Not that anyone noticed. Ryan grimaced. *Nova's brand of inherited magic was awful, and it was made worse by their parents' narcissistic neglect. It still made Ryan's blood boil that no one had tried to teach Nova how to use their power. Everything Nova and Ryan learned was from weird books long forgotten in library stacks.*

And still, they had never discovered how to control it. Just that it existed, it was rare, and most who displayed talent with it didn't survive. Every time Nova found a new book, their shoulders would straighten, and their aura would light up, but by the end of every text, some of the stars had winked out, and their shoulders had been pulled forward by grief.

"FUCK!" Ryan sat bolt upright in his memory, and his eyes whipped open. He sat on his bed and watched as his memories of Nova, the journal, and the infernal knowledge it had given them were sucked away in a vacuum of singing and shrieking.

"Don't wake up. Don't wake up. Whatever is out there is worse than this. Stay here," I kept telling myself, willing my unconsciousness to continue.

And it worked, until…

*

I landed. Hard.

My eyes flew open as splinters of pain ricocheted up my legs.

I blinked into the darkness of the cave. "H-h-hello?"

Silence.

"Where am I?" I looked around. I was close to the mouth of a cave; I started to scramble toward to the dim light, but a hand closed around my ankle and yanked me backward.

My pained scream was met with harsh laughter. "I'm not finished with you yet."

Tears fell on the sandy earth beneath me. "Please let me go."

I turned onto my side, and my eyes fell on the face of a girl with a blue bandana loosely tied around her neck. The edges of the bandana were stained with a rusty red that made the fabric look a dirty purple. "Blood! She's bleeding! Help her!" I yelled and scrambled back.

More laughter. "I don't think she'll notice." My captor bent over and lifted the head by her hair.

I laid my head on my arms and began to sob. "I don't understand. What's happening to me? Where am I?"

My head was jerked back, and a woman with black eyes ringed with a thin band of emerald green whispered into my face, "You're about to die."

"What?"

The woman let go of my hair and spun around. "Who's there?" she demanded.

I squinted and could see a weird grey smudge gliding around the cave. "What is that?" I whispered.

She pulled me to my feet; I whimpered at the pain shooting up my ankles. "What? What did you see?" the woman asked.

Out of my peripheral vision, I could see the smudge getting closer and taking shape. It almost looked like a person, but it was very out of focus. "Nothing. I have dirt in my eye."

The creature threw me farther into the cave, farther from any chance of escape. I landed with a clatter onto a pile of...

"BONES!" My voice echoed loudly in the cave.

The creature stalked over to me and kneeled down. "Well, I had to sleep on something."

Footsteps scurried behind the wings of my monster. "Hades! What is in here?" She stood and looked back at the mouth of the cave.

"Ry, I'm here. I'm not leaving you," a disembodied voice hissed into my ear.

Ry? Am I Ry? I chanced a glace in the direction of the voice, but it was too dark where I was. I couldn't see anything.

"No, don't look at me. Don't say anything. Don't react at all. I am going to get her away from you. Then you need to run. Fast."

I nodded. I didn't want to tell the voice that I couldn't run. I kept my eyes glued to the beast pacing the cave. Her wings flared out behind her as she looked for the phantom that seemed determined to help me get away. I could only hope that whoever it was got far enough away that they wouldn't see my undoing. I wasn't going anywhere.

My eyes widened as I saw the grey spot slide across the mouth of the cave, and all of a sudden, one of the creature's wings was stretched out; a feather was then plucked and thrown in the air. She whirled, but there was nothing but laughter in the air as the raven feather flitted in a downward spiral. Next, I watched her head snap back as though her hair had been pulled.

"Catch me if you can." Dust flew into the air as my savior took off, the monster hot on the trail.

I closed my eyes and breathed in. "One. Two. Three." Then I exhaled just as slowly. I had to give my spirit friend time to get away. They could not know I was never going to escape.

After a few minutes, I crawled out of the nest of bones. I wanted to be outside one last time. I pulled myself forward with exhausted arms and useless legs and sighed with relief as the sun and fresh forest air hit my face. I looked around, but didn't see anyone.

Hope suddenly bloomed in my chest. Could I get somewhere? I had no idea where I was, or how I got out here, but maybe I could find some help. I continued to pull myself forward agonizingly. I was almost to the waterline when she landed in front of me.

She folded herself down so that she could be eye to eye with me. Tilting her head this way and that, she smiled, revealing two rows of glistening fangs. "Why chase what I can't see, when I have a perfectly good, busted bird right in front of me?"

I laid my head down and sent a message to the universe to protect those who had tried to save me.

THE NEST
AN INTERLUDE

Nova stood in the trees and watched in horror as their best friend—*My only friend*, Nova thought—lay crumpled on the ground while two monsters fought over him. Aggie had dropped her shawl, and as she circled Ryan, Nova saw jagged scars that started at Aggie's shoulder blades and made their way down her ribs in a lightning pattern. And down her arms hung droopy grey feathers that matched the ones that Nova had been collecting.

Aggie was singing, and her adversary was shrieking; the effect was so nauseating that Nova had difficulty concentrating. They looked down at Ryan, watched as his fists clenched and unclenched.

Is he still unconscious? Does he know what is happening? Will he be like the rest?

"No." It couldn't be; they would do everything in their power to make sure that Ryan came through this, even if he couldn't remember anything.

Suddenly...

Silence.

Nova blinked. *What is happening now?*

They still stood over Ryan, now both completely out of breath and glaring at each other.

Nova stepped forward, and a twig snapped underfoot. Aggie's eyes darted right at Nova. The other, seeing an opportunity, took flight with Ryan. Immediately, Aggie started singing again.

Nova tried to follow the flight path.

"You can't save him, you know."

Nova glared at Aggie. "I am coming back for you."

Aggie shrugged. "If we meet again, I'll be ready."

Nova nodded and took off running.

*

Nova stood at the mouth of the cave, watching their friend sob in the dirt. They needed a plan. A plan so Ryan could get away. This was the only thing they could do to repay him for all those years of being there, helping, consoling, and just being a friend. They looked at the monster who stood laughing over their friend.

Then they saw it. Marissa's head. Just her head. The creature lifted it as if it were some kind of game. This beast had killed their friend. Nova looked deeper in the cave, and lying a few feet away from Ryan's feet was a leg with an infected tattoo on the ankle.

"John!" Nova gasped.

"Who's there?" Her voice was rough.

Ryan looked at Nova. "What's that?"

Nova's heart sank; Ryan couldn't see them anymore. At least not all of them. Nope, it didn't matter; they were going to get Ryan out of here.

Ryan gave Nova the side-eye and claimed that he saw nothing. Nova couldn't be sure if Ryan meant it, or if he was trying to protect them, even though he had no reason to. Nova covered their ears at the screech that echoed off the stone walls and watched Ryan land in a nest of bones.

Slowly, they crept over to him. *"Ry, I'm here. I'm not leaving you."* When Ryan tried to catch Nova's eye, they kept talking. *"No, don't look at me. Don't say anything. Don't react at all. I am going to get her away from you. Then you need to run. Fast."* Ryan's slight nod was all Nova needed.

They walked over to the beast and pulled on her wing, and then pulled her hair. Nova threw dust in the air so that they would be seen running. Nova booked it. They made sure to make as much noise as possible. Kicking every rock, stepping on every stick, and shouting. They made so much noise that it took much longer than it should have to realize that they weren't being followed anymore.

Nova turned back and ran toward the cave. *Ryan. I have to get back to Ryan,* they thought, legs pumping in time with the mantra of their friend's name.

The trees opened to the lake, and there was Ryan, lying on the ground. For the first time, Nova noticed that his ankles and feet were bent at unnatural angles. Why hadn't he said anything? Nova watched as the bird-woman landed and crouched in front of Ryan.

"Come on, Ry. Keep her talking. I'm coming."

Nova skidded to a halt as they watched the monster hold Ryan in the air with one hand and slice him open from stomach to throat with the other. Then she closed her midnight wings around them both. Nova screamed.

The black wings opened, and all that was left were some scraps, bones, and the blood that stained the monster's face. She stood and turned in Nova's general direction. "When you see my sister again, thank her for me. I never have gotten so much to eat so easily before." With that, she unfurled her wings completely and ascended above the trees. One final horrifying screech filled the air, and the rest was...

Silence.

Nova was left alone.

PART IV

The Invisible

Rigid Resentment.
Red-Hot Rage.
Ready to scorch anyone who
Comes near your shattered
Inner child.
No one saw you.
No one acknowledged you.
Now is your time.
Reveal yourself.

Nova

I left him. I left my best friend.

One foot in front of the other.

There was nothing I could do for him. For any of us. No one listened. Ever.

They never listen!

Keep walking. Don't stop. You're the only one left.

Why did we ever stop at the damned fire? Why did we come out here without protection spells? Why did I come back at all?

I stumbled. "Whoa there. Keep it together. You have to keep it together."

I looked up. It was dark. When had night fallen? Night had fallen, and my best friend was back there. Alone.

Dead. They were all dead.

"Not me. I survived. Stupid, stupid family magic. Stupid family for not caring. Not noticing. Stupid Ryan." I felt the first tear fall then.

"Stupid. Stupid Ryan."

More tears.

I fell to my knees, and then I heard it. Aggie's song.

I looked up. "Time to end this."

1890

Over the river
And through the woods,
She's off to save her friend.

*

"Once upon a time, there was a young girl who left home to save her best friend from the Snow Queen. Along the way, she veered off the path from her quest and was taken in by a witch. The witch promised the girl that she could have anything if she would just stay with her in a never-ending summer and garden that had every flower she could imagine. Days of doing whatever she wanted. And in return, the witch would have what she had always wanted—companionship.

"And the girl stayed. She was taken in by the clear days, the candy-like fragrance of all the flowers, and she soon forgot about her best friend. She played in the fields of wildflowers. Made friends with bees and butterflies. She would take naps in the fields with bunnies that whispered sweet bedtime stories to her.

"And in time, the girl learned that she also had magic within her. She could name every flower and the significance behind each one. She knew, for instance, that marigolds were the guardians of any garden they were planted around, and that they also represented the death of a loved one; the witch had one part of her garden walled off, and along the smooth top, sat pots of marigolds. In the sunset, that part of the garden looked as if it were on fire. It was the one part of the garden that the young girl was not allowed to visit. And since that was the only rule she had been given, she followed it.

"One day while the girl was walking near the gate at the edge of the summer garden, she found a rosebush. On the one bush, there were roses of all colors. The young girl recognized the magic in that; she picked only the yellow ones that meant friendship and took the witch a bouquet.

"The witch recoiled at the sight of the flowers, and in her anger, the magic shattered. Everything that was holding the girl in the forever summer was wiped away. Suddenly, the girl remembered her best friend and the quest she had been on.

"The girl bent down to pick up the flowers and discovered that the hands that reached out in front of her weren't a child's hands. But a woman's. She stood, the flowers forgotten, trying to understand whose hands she was looking at. She wouldn't know until much later, but she had been in the witch's garden for almost ten years.

"The young woman fled the garden, left her witch, and rescued her best friend from the Snow Queen. And they lived happily ever after."

The little girl bounced with excitement. This was her favorite bedtime story. Her brother, on the other hand, hated fairy tales. "Grandma, come on. That never happened," he said.

Cathleen rolled her eyes; boys were so odd. Her hazel eyes big and round, she looked at her grandma. "But it did so. You said. It did happen, didn't it?" Cathleen knew that magic was real, and she knew that her grandmother would never lie to her.

Gerta smiled at her grandchildren. "It is true, more or less."

Robert smirked at Cathleen. "See? I told you. It's fake."

Cathleen's eyes filled with tears, and Gerta scooped her up. "Robert, I didn't say that. I said 'more or less.' That means that I told my truth of the tale, but there are parts to the story that, if I told them, would take the truth away from the others that were involved."

Gerta didn't tell the children that the parts of her story she never talked about, not even to Kay, were too traumatic to put into words. She never talked about how the witch had brutalized her, so angry and terrified of the roses that she beat Gerta until she thought she would die. Gerta never learned what it was about the roses that had set the witch off; moreover, Gerta could never reconcile that the woman she had come to love as a sister, the one she had believed was the only person in the world who loved her, was really a bloodthirsty witch.

*

After beating Gerta and leaving her bleeding in the reeds, the witch stalked back to her house to get a knife to finish the job. Before going, though, she knelt down next to Gerta, looked into her swollen eyes, and said, "You had better be here when I get back. If you move from this spot, when I find you, I will kill you more slowly than you could dream possible."

Gerta lay on the cold ground, shaking in fear and pain; she rolled onto her back and looked toward the rosebush. She saw that it was snowing outside of the garden, and that meant she had a way out. Gerta crawled to the rosebush, focusing all of her thoughts on Kay. Knowing that he was still out there alone gave Gerta the determination to fight for her escape. Somehow, she found the strength to crawl out of the nightmarish summer and into the reality of winter.

Out of the witch's clutches, she was saved by the kindly Mr. and Mrs. Crow, who helped her heal and find new shoes, as she had left her childish red ones in the garden. With their help, and that of the friends she made along the way, Gerta was able to complete her quest and get her best friend back.

*

Neither Kay nor Gerta made it through their trials without scars. Gerta thought back to the moments in their life together when Kay would go so cold she thought he was dying. She watched his face turn blue and lips turn to frost. All she could do was hold him tightly in her arms until he was warm again.

Together, they had made a beautiful family. Scars and all.

*

Along the way,
The girl lost her way
And became trapped in
Sun and flowers.

*

Kay found Gerta kneeling in her garden the next day. He had come looking for her, following the sound of singing that he believed to be Gerta singing to herself. However, when he found her, she was leaning forward, her hands braced in the dirt, and she was completely rigid, her eyes blank.

Kay looked around for where the singing was coming from, but he couldn't see anything. He shook off the nervous feeling he had, leaned over, and touched Gerta's shoulder.

Gerta blinked. "Oh my, I must have been dazed." Gerta sat back on her heels and rolled her shoulders to relieve her stiff back from all the weeding she had done.

"You know, the boys would be more than happy to do that for you."

Gerta smiled up at Kay. "I know, but I like it. Besides, the last time they weeded my garden, my basil and sage mysteriously vanished."

Kay chuckled and laid his hands on Gerta's slim shoulders. "I know, but you know you're the only one who can remember what all of these plants are, and which ones don't belong. I don't know how you do it. But, you know, their mistake still saved you days of shoulder and back pain."

Gerta stood and wiped her hands on her apron. "I'm all done for today, I promise."

Kay smiled, brushed a steel-colored strand of hair out of Gerta's eyes, and kissed her gently. His lips were cold. "Let's get you to the fire. I'll make soup for dinner."

Gerta brought Kay's soup to the fire, where he was bent under the weight of all his blankets. These moments always scared Gerta the most; she never knew when Kay was going to go cold, and the truly unnerving part was Kay never knew either. When it happened, though, they dealt with it with as little discussion as possible, and when Kay warmed again, he never acknowledged that the episode had ever happened. Gerta didn't feel right about pushing the conversation, either, because she had her own secrets.

On her good days, Gerta felt bad for the witch, exiled to a garden alone, waiting for visitors to stay with her. On her bad days, she remembered the years she lost there, and felt nothing but hatred for the witch who'd kidnapped her and let her believe that all they had in the world was each other. The reality was that she had lost ten years in that infernal garden. It was no wonder that she knew the names of every plant and flower in the world. It wasn't magic after all, just years of learning and relearning their names and meanings.

As Kay sipped his soup, Gerta laid a hand on his back and rubbed gently. Gerta thought back to the day she finally found Kay.

*

Gerta had been traveling for weeks, stopping and asking if anyone remembered seeing a boy some years before. At every town and travelers' stop she came across, there was always at least one person who remembered seeing a young boy traveling by sleigh, which was pulled by polar bears and left an icy trail in its wake. Next to the young boy had been a statuesque woman dressed in icy blue. Her white hair had been piled on top of her head, a diamond tiara holding it in place.

Gerta followed the decade-old trail until she found the ice palace. She slid across the frozen moat and pushed her way into the castle. Everything was made of ice and snow, and Gerta shivered when she walked through the main hall, which was lined with statues of men in different horrific positions.

Who would pose for such grotesque art?

Gerta continued forward and found herself in the throne room, facing the queen. And there was Kay, sitting next to the queen's throne like a pet. This Kay, though, looked different. Time had passed for him as well, and he had grown into an adult. Gerta had to work to see her childhood friend in the frozen trophy before her.

To buy Kay's freedom, the Queen gave Gerta and Kay a puzzle to solve. Kay couldn't move the pieces—his hands were so frozen—but Gerta's warm hands thawed the pieces enough to place them and complete the puzzle.

The Snow Queen was furious, but kept her end of the deal; they were freed.

*

Kay was frozen through and sitting in front of the fire; Gerta was sobbing and apologizing to Kay's grandmother over and over again. She knew that she could never make up for the time Kay's grandmother had lost before Gerta found him. She laid her head in his lap and sobbed until she was empty and his legs were soaked.

Kay rested a frozen hand on her head, and he whispered, "You should not have come for me."

Gerta was sure that she had misheard him, but when she looked up into Kay's eyes and saw how stone-cold they were, she wondered if he was right. Maybe she had been too late. She kept her eyes locked on his and watched as they thawed from frozen slate grey back to the warm hazel she remembered so well.

She squinted slightly as something in the corner of his eye caught the light of the fire. Glass, he had a glass shard in his eye. She'd missed it because he had been made of ice when she got to him. Now that he was thawing, the sliver was much easier to see. It was plain to Gerta that it was glass, not a shard of ice, sticking out of Kay's eye. She reached up and gently slid it out of his tear duct.

In that moment, Kay warmed completely and smiled at Gerta as if not a day had passed.

*

Now, though, Gerta wondered if she had gotten all of the glass out of Kay's eye that day. Maybe that was why he still got cold; maybe there was more glass lodged somewhere.

"Here, I'm finished." Kay handed Gerta the empty bowl. The bottom of it was covered in a thin film of frost where he had held it.

"Thank you. I'll wash it." Gerta turned toward the kitchen.

Kay suddenly grabbed her arm; his hand was an icy grey. "Gerta. I love you; thank you for saving me. You keep my heart warm."

Gerta smiled, reassured that their love was the kind of fairy tales and that when she told her grandchildren, "Happily ever after," she knew it to be the truest part of the story.

"I love you too. Why don't you sleep here in front of the fire? You are especially cold tonight."

"Yes, I think that's a great idea." Kay stood and started to make a pallet for himself on the hearth.

Gerta stopped at the base of the stairs to say good night, but Kay was already asleep. It broke Gerta's heart to see the pile of blankets shivering.

*

Over the river,
Through the woods,
He's off to find his queen.

*

Gerta sat up straight in bed. She could have sworn that she heard music, but that was absurd because they only had a piano in the house and what she'd heard was a woman singing and playing some other sort of instrument. They didn't have a phonograph; maybe Gerta had been dreaming. She was settling herself back in bed when she heard the door open and shut.

Gerta went to her window and looked out. "Kay!" she shouted.

He turned, and in the moonlight, Kay looked as frozen as he had been the day she arrived at the Snow Queen's palace.

In her slippers and nightgown, Gerta ran down the stairs and out into the night. "Kay!" she shouted again.

He kept walking forward, his movements slow and rigid, as though his joints were frozen.

Gerta finally caught up with Kay and stood in front of him. "What are you doing? Where are you going?"

Kay didn't even look down at her when he said, "Home. To my queen."

Gerta stood her ground as he tried to push past her. "No, your home is with me. Your wife. I saved you from that frozen hell a lifetime ago."

Kay finally looked at Gerta. His eyes were round ice cubes, and they shot daggers into her heart. "No, she saved me from a lifetime of pain. I don't even know who you are."

"I told you; I am your wife. I am the one who keeps your heart warm," she said, echoing the words he had used that same evening.

Kay looked down his nose at her and then looked away, into the distance, dismissing Gerta.

Gerta fell to the ground, her chest heaving. All that work, all that love, gone. Kay stepped around her and lumbered down the road. Gerta watched him go, not knowing if he would find the Snow Queen again, or if she would take him back if he returned; she did know that she was too old to save him again.

Once Kay was out of sight, Gerta pushed to her feet and started to numbly walk home. She tripped on a loose cobblestone, and a gloved hand gripped her arm.

"Steady there."

Gerta looked up into a smiling face. "Thank you, miss."

The woman made sure Gerta was steady before adjusting her gloves and cloak. "No need for thanks. I'm just glad that I happened to be here."

"Well, I appreciate the coincidence."

The woman smiled again, and Gerta noticed that the smile did not quite reach her cold green eyes. "You wouldn't happen to know the way back to the inn, would you? I arrived in town late yesterday and have lost my way. Thank goodness, we came across each other; not many people are awake this late to assist a lady in need."

Gerta rubbed her arm. "Yes, of course. Just continue down this lane, and you'll come right into town. The inn is off of the main street, on Stoney Place."

"Thank you." And the woman walked off into the dark, humming quietly.

Nova

*T*he tree itself is nothing to look at; it's small, and the tips of the drooping branches are rotted from the constant water dripping from them. There is a pool at the base of the tree; that is what I am here for.

When I arrive at the clearing, I stop in awe. The glow from the full moon lights the pool; it looks like the silver of a mirror. The droplets glisten like glitter in the air.

It has taken me years to find this tree. And now that I'm here, I can't believe how small and insignificant it looks. In the journal my dad gave me, the tree was described as powerful and magnificent; I assumed that meant it was grandiose, and its branches covered the sky. This sad little willow tree is shorter than I am. But I can feel the magic radiating out of the pool with every silvery tear that falls from its branches.

Slowly, I step into the clearing. The air changes. It is cooler and cleaner. I take a deep breath, and everything becomes clear. I am supposed to be here; finally, I have found where I belong. Now, it won't matter that no one remembers me. That no one sees me— "Except Ryan," I say to myself mournfully. All that matters is soon I'll know everyone's secrets.

And they will pay.

More confidently, I stride forward and kneel at the pool. From the bag at my hip, I pull a leather-bound journal. Gently, I lift the brown ribbon to open the page I marked. Looking down, I start to *recite the Gratitude Prayer that was a constant in every text I unearthed about this tree. If I am going to do this with as few consequences as possible, I need to do it right.*

Setting the journal down, I pull a purple candle and lighter from my bag. I press the base of the candle into the soft dirt in front of me and light it. The candle's glow is dim in comparison to the silver lights floating all around me.

Deep breath in.

Relax your jaw, and drop your shoulders.

Deep breath out.

Feel yourself grounded in the earth.

I take this offering with gratitude.
I will use its gifts with conscious intent.
As the flame of this candle burns constant and true,
So shall the knowledge that it will imbue.

I open my eyes and watch as the water dripping from the branches stops. It is waiting for me to drink. I pull one final thing from my bag. A clear goblet with a pewter stem. Slowly, I reach out toward the small pool and dip the goblet into its water. I put the cup to my lips and drink. The water turns to ash in my mouth. My reaction is to spit it out, but I have to finish this. I swallow hard.

When the goblet is empty, the branches start dripping water down into the pool again. The splashes are enough to extinguish the candle, just as all those who have done the ritual before said it would. I slowly pack the goblet, candle, lighter, and journal back into my bag. With a final thanks, I stand and leave the clearing.

I feel changed, and that change gives me a confidence I have never felt before. This is when my life starts. I smile and continue forward.

*

My eyes snapped open. I was splayed out facedown on the ground; the singing had stopped. The sun was coming up; I had survived the night.

"Dammit." I pushed slowly to my feet. That witch couldn't have gotten far. She didn't have the wings to get that far. I dusted myself off and started forward. I needed to find a trail; I needed to get back to the highway.

I felt my anger start to rise as I walked. The clearer my head became, the angrier I got.

Ryan had hiked these trails since he was kid, and he swore he knew exactly where he was going. And for a while, he did. They smiled at the memory of Ryan pointing out a tree that he and his parents had always "marked" when they came here, and of Ryan and John upholding that tradition. Then Ryan's constant chatter slowed, and finally stopped when he realized that they were lost. "My compass is spinning," he had said. Still, we had soldiered on, believing that we would find the campsite. It was all a fun jaunt before graduation. I knew why John had pushed this trip. I knew what he was.

That had happened before I got back, but when I saw John, the invisible ink he sported screamed into my face. He was his family's StoryKeeper; it was supposed to be Zelda, but she died. I cringed when I remembered feeling, beyond a shadow of a doubt, that John thought Zelda's death was a suicide. StoryKeeping is a doomed life, one that is best passed on as late in life as possible. This trip was rushed, and John had already been reeling from the pressure of generations of tradition scarred into his skin.

I kept his secret.

He lost his life.

Marissa had no such secrets. She was just… "Repressed," I said out loud to break the crushing silence around me as I walked. When I got back, she was still the same angry, scared Marissa. She died fighting.

Ryan. He was waiting at the airport when I got back from…from… "Where the hell did I go?" I searched my memory. Nothing. I stopped walking and closed my eyes. I got the journal from my dad. I still didn't know what finally made him remember he had a child at all, let alone one with this kind of power. Ryan helped me research everything in the journal, including the…

"Tree! I went to the tree!" That had to be it, but where was the memory of the traveling? I took a deep breath and searched my memory further; there was something there in its place. It felt strange and uncomfortable, a memory that didn't quite fit, one that wasn't mine.

*

An older couple. The man has something wrong with him. Something that is lodged in his heart. A magic that was placed there intentionally. To call him home when it was time.

I smiled and ran my tongue along my teeth. It was time. I sang to them both; I couldn't have her saving him as I returned him to his rightful place.

Oh, this woman was in so much pain; she had been so afraid that this would happen someday. How delicious. I watched as she chased her frozen husband down the street. She tried to stop him, to remind him of the warmth, of home. He pushed her to the ground.

I was smiling as I walked up to her. To help her up. And to ask for directions. She helped me; she's a nice lady. It's a shame I had to take her husband from her. But it was time for him to take his rightful place next to his queen.

*

I blinked. This was an old memory, older than this century. How strange to have a memory taken from me, and this one put in its place. I shook my head. Whose memory was it?

I started walking again; I still had to get out of here. I had to tell everyone's families what happened.

Did I, though? I ran my hands through my gritty hair. None of the families would even know who I am, and when the newspapers reported this, there's no way they would even mention me. Why couldn't I just disappear and leave everyone to wonder, to not know? I sighed heavily. Because *I* would know. And Ryan would know. Even though he was gone, knowing I would disappoint him again wasn't something I could bear.

I looked around to get my bearings. Well, I was on a real trail again, so thank God for small favors. I was bound to run into some people at some point or another; it wasn't like the Pacific Crest Trail was abandoned.

I chuckled dryly to myself. "Then where were all the people these past few days? I hate magic!"

"Oh, you do, do you?"

I swung around. "How did you find me?"

Aggie held her hands out. "I've been following you since I sang last night."

"I have something of yours, you know."

Aggie started. "What?"

"Think really hard. What did you sing last night?" I asked, finally realizing what we had been dealing with this whole time.

Aggie's scrunched up her face as she tried to remember. "All I can see is that tree. Where is my story?"

"Oh, Jesus. Aren't we a pair? You a Siren. And me...a SecretStealer."

"A what? I've never heard of that."

"I'm sure you haven't."

"No matter. I'll find out what it is."

"At what cost?" I thought back to the memory she had sung from me. Or, at least, to the spot in which that memory used to be held. I remembered everything that led up to that misfit memory that had somehow inserted itself in my brain. How silly I had been. I was going to be a spy. I had everything figured out—I would go, taking the journal and all the maps with me. Ryan would, of course, come with me, keep me grounded, and I was going to make all those people who ignored me pay.

Ryan didn't go with me. He had drawn that line in the sand, had stood up for himself. I went alone. And then… nothing…until I got back.

"It's no matter; I have hundreds of stories. I have more stories than you have years to your life."

"I'm sure you do, but are you sure you understand the cost of losing those memories? Of giving your secrets to me?"

Aggie laughed. "You assume I actually want these memories."

I shrugged. "I don't assume anything anymore. I only know what I've seen happen to my friends, and what I've seen you take."

Aggie awkwardly adjusted the lute on her back. "What happened to you?"

"I made choices." And because of those choices, I was growing more burned-out every day. Burned-out after being let down by people I looked up to, tired of holding on to the darkest corners of people's souls. I thought of Ryan; he was the only one who didn't let me down. Not even at the end, after Aggie had taken everything from him; Ryan was at his core a pure soul. And I let him down.

When I got back from my adventure, Ryan was waiting at the airport. His face fell when he saw me; it shamed me that he could see what I had done. I knew I wouldn't be able to hide it from him, but it was the first time in my life that I actively wished to be invisible to him. Still, he was the only one who didn't radiate secrets. My whole trip home was full of things that I didn't want to know. And the more people tried to hide from their intrusion, the louder they streamed into my brain.

I fell into Ryan's arms and sobbed. My whole body had been overwhelmed by people and their secrets. They were everywhere, and I had no boundaries. Once again, I only had a portion of the information I actually needed. I had been so focused on getting back at people, on getting my just desserts, that I had become just this shell of pain and misery.

This was the part that was missing from the journal; no one wrote about the "after." Why had no one talked about the consequences? The scariest thought of all was that maybe there hadn't been consequences for those who had come before me. Maybe they had all been so sadistic that everyone omitted what I now knew was the most important part—the price of knowing everyone's secrets. Especially since I didn't have anyone to hold on to mine. Instead of being the greatest spy, I found myself wanting to be "Mr. Cellophane." But for real this time.

"Choices? *Choices*?" Aggie asked, interrupting my thoughts. "You know I can see you now. I don't know how this whole thing works yet, but I do know, from our friend Ryan, that you were not always this way. So I ask again. What did that tree do to you?"

I scrubbed my hands over my face and into my hair, making it stand on end. "I don't know. I *cannot* remember. You took that. All I know is before…and after. And the after? So much worse than I ever considered during the before." I locked eyes with Aggie. "Why are you doing this to us? Why did you choose us?"

"Honestly? You entered the circle I cast. It could have been anyone out there, but once you all walked into it, it was sealed to anyone else."

I leaned back against a tree and laughed mirthlessly. "I have lost my one friend, and his friends, because of …chance?"

"Sometimes, that's all it is."

I pushed off the tree and wrapped my hands around Aggie's throat. I squeezed as tight as I could, until I felt my fingers meet at the back of her neck.

Her face turned beet red, but she didn't fight me. In fact, she looked amused. I kept squeezing, and a smile slowly spread across her face. Her hand snaked up and grabbed the front of my flannel shirt. Without any effort, she threw me off her. "Do you feel better?" she asked me.

I pushed to my knees and tried to catch my breath. "No, I never feel better. I never feel anything. I am so tired."

Aggie crossed over to me, squatted down, and tilted my chin up to look me in the eyes. "Let me help you with that. I can take all of that away."

I jerked my face away. "Don't. Don't be fake now. You're going to take my *stories*, no matter what, so just do it."

Aggie sat back and rested her arms on her knees. "You and Ryan, so resigned to your fates. Although, through it all, Ryan was trying to protect you. And you…what? You're just ready to give it all up?"

"Yes, I am," I said, wishing this were over. *Come on, Aggie, sing already. I'm ready. Let's just do this.*

"What was that? What happened?" Aggie asked, looking at me strangely.

"What?" I looked around.

"Your color, it…rippled."

"Rippled?"

"Yeah, and now I feel all edgy and impatient."

"Listen, I don't have the bandwidth to help you figure out your powers. I can barely manage mine."

"Don't I know it. Have you seen what you're carrying with you?"

"I don't need to see what I'm carrying. I feel it. All the time."

"Aren't they heavy?"

"And getting heavier," I quipped, although I had to admit Aggie had piqued my interest.

Aggie shrugged. "It's your burden, I guess, but, goddess, you look miserable."

"I am miserable. And exhausted. I don't want to play these games anymore. Can we finish this? I'm ready to forget all of this."

Aggie lifted her lute and strummed softly. "That, I can promise you."

800 BCE

My charge,
My ward,
My friend,
I follow you blindly
Into the blackest depths.

*

Aglaope gulped as she descended slowly the obsidian stairs and entered the swirling fog. She always hated this part and swore that this was the last time she would ever come down here. Aglaope looked back over her shoulder to make sure that nothing had taken notice that she was missing.

Persephone would never let the secret be known. They were too close to the end now. But if they got caught. *Ha! If,* Aglaope thought. She *knew* that they were going to get caught, but it wouldn't be Persephone who was brought before the High Court. It would be Aglaope.

"Fifty-six, fifty-seven, fifty-eight..." She was counting the steps down because the air itself was black in the UnderWorld.

At the bottom of the stairway, sticky fog swam around her feet. Aglaope adjusted the medallion at the top of her dress and stepped up to the iron gate. Like everything else down here, it was black; yet, by some magic, it stood out like a beacon to souls.

"Your passage fee?" a dusty voice whispered as a skeletal hand unfolded from the bars of the gate.

Aglaope slid the parchment and coins into Charon's hand.

His skull fell forward. "Again?"

Aglaope nodded nervously. *He will still deliver the letter, won't he? Goddess, let this be quick so that I can escape this eternal blackness and go back AboveWorld.*

Charon rolled his head as though he had eyes to roll. "You know, Aglaope. This is getting really old."

"Yes, I know. It is for me too. You are going to send this along, aren't you?"

"As though I have a choice. It'll have to wait until a soul is ready to cross, though."

Aglaope bowed her head. "Of course, milord. My lady blesses your courage."

"Your lady is nothing to me."

She nodded, head still bowed.

"Look at me, child."

Aglaope raised her head as Charon leaned farther out of the gate he lived in while waiting for souls to beg passage.

"Be careful. You do not serve who you think you do. It is your head on the block when this goes sideways."

"Yes, milord."

"Go. Leave this place. Before it leaves permanent marks on you."

Aglaope needed no further invitation; she turned on her heel and flew back up the stairs and into the sun.

*

You, who would sacrifice
Your very family
To get what you
Desire
(Power),
Think nothing of what
I risk.

*

Aglaope found her mistress and sisters basking together under the shade of an enormous apple tree. She slowed her breathing and walked toward them as naturally as possible.

"There you are!" Persephone trilled.

Peisinoe plucked a grape from an ornate silver bowl that was overflowing with fruit. "Where have you been?"

"Probably meeting up with some…mortal," the youngest sister sneered, shielding her eyes from the sun with a delicate hand as she looked up at Aglaope.

Aglaope smiled tightly. "Yes, that's it. You know me so well. I am always going off with some mortal."

Persephone pouted. "Aglaope, how can you ensure my safety if you're always running off?"

Aglaope grimaced. "Apologies, milady."

"Well, you're here now, and I'm sure that your sisters would like a break as they've been pulling double duty all morning while you were out gallivanting."

Thelxiepeia stood up and shook out her lavender dress. "Thank goddess." She strode out from under the yawning branches, into a clearing, stretched out her massive crow wings, and launched into the sky.

Peisinoe stayed firmly planted on the grass, glued to Persephone's side. "I don't think it's a good idea to leave you so completely unprotected. Who knows when Aglaope will become...distracted again."

Persephone patted Peisinoe's hand. "Now, dear, we'll be fine for a few moments. Please go; stretch your legs."

Reluctantly, Peisinoe stood, her blinding-white wings stretching as she walked off, but Aglaope noticed that she stopped and set up a vantage point just barely out of earshot of Persephone.

Aglaope adjusted her skirts so that they wouldn't become entangled with her talons and sat down next to her charge.

"Goddess, but your sisters are a bore."

Aglaope tucked a curl behind her ear and kept scanning the area. "We are only here to keep you safe. Not. Entertained."

"Chaste. You mean chaste." Persephone's voice had deepened; she no longer sounded as though she were a child.

"I suppose I did mean that, yes."

"Is there any word back?"

"Not this time."

Persephone sat up and started pulling out grass.

"Don't do that. Your mother hates it."

Persephone smiled humorlessly. "I know."

Aglaope nodded slightly and looked over at Peisinoe, then up at Thelxiepeia, who was soaring in the sky, happy to be free. "Do you understand the risk of what I'm doing for you?"

Persephone frowned. "You'll keep delivering my letters? Until this is over, right?"

Aglaope noticed Persephone didn't answer the question. "I gave you my word. But I need your word back that when this ends, my sisters will not be included in whatever punishment is brought down."

Persephone placed her small hand over her heart and said, "My word as my father's niece."

Aglaope looked at Persephone. "Yes, *that's* believable."

They both laughed then, Persephone in true jest and Aglaope to assuage her own guilt over betraying her sisters.

*

I hold your masks
As you reveal
Your true self
To no one.
(How foolish I've been.)

*

"Please. Just this last one. I need to know that he is coming for sure." Persephone grabbed Aglaope's arm and squeezed.

"I can't keep going down there. Charon said that the last letter I took for you is all you need. Please. I cannot do this again." Aglaope wrenched her arm free and went to the window to keep watch.

"I cannot stay here another minute. I have to get out of here."

Aglaope crossed her arms and gripped them before turning to face Persephone. "I am going to get you out of here. But you have to be patient. You have done all this careful planning; let's just let it ride for a few more days. Then, I promise, I will go back down there and get your message to Hades."

Persephone's face turned grey, and then her cheeks flushed in anger. "No one speaks to me this way. I am leaving. One way or another."

Aglaope left the window and stood face-to-face with the petulant goddess. "Do you hear yourself? Were you even listening to me? Everything is going according to plan. You will be free of them soon. I am not speaking to you in any way, other than to say no."

Persephone was a statue. "Fine. Yes. Of course. I hear you. I shouldn't have asked you in the first place. We will wait."

Aglaope squinted at Persephone suspiciously. "Yes. We will wait." She turned and walked back to the window. Aglaope inhaled deeply. Charon was right. This was not going to end well.

*

Your intentions
Were never true.
Still I followed you.
Empty promises.
False hopes.
Still I believed
In you.

*

The next morning, Aglaope awoke with the sun cutting a blazing crease across her eyelids. As she blinked the sleep away, she heard voices outside the bedroom. Immediately at attention, she ran to Persephone's bed.

Empty.

"Hades and damnation!"

"Why are you shouting on such a beautiful morning?" Persephone asked lightly, walking in with a tray of nectar and ambrosia.

Aglaope slumped against the wall in relief. "Who were you talking to out there?"

"Hmm? Oh, Hermes came by with a message from Mother."

"And you received it?" *Great. I'll never hear the end of this from Peisinoe.* "What was the message?"

Persephone waved the question away. "Nothing important. Now, come and eat. You were so worn out last night from your jaunt that I took pity on you and let you sleep. Don't worry. We'll just add this to our list of little secrets."

"Yes, I suppose we will," Aglaope said doubtfully. She sat down at the small table and began to eat breakfast.

Later that day, Persephone and her guards went for a walk along the shore. They walked in silence for a long while, Persephone picking up shells and then discarding them as she found more things that caught her eye. The three sisters kept vigilant around her.

As Persephone was throwing another shell down, she said casually, "Let's go see if Orpheus is playing. Please, it's been so long since I've danced."

"Milady, that is not a good idea. You know the Satyrs always slip something into the wine to turn it," Peisinoe responded.

Persephone stuck out her bottom lip. "Please. We won't drink the wine. Not a drop. Please."

Peisinoe rolled her eyes at her sisters, and Aglaope held firm. "You heard Peisinoe, and she's right. It is not a good idea. Let us just continue our walk, and then we'll go for a swim."

"What is the sense of having guardians if we can't go see anyone?"

Thelxiepeia shook Aglaope's arm. "Yes, come on. It will be so much fun to see our friends again. And at the first sign of trouble, we'll fly Persephone out of there." She twitched her wings coquettishly.

Wavering, Peisinoe said, "You swear you won't drink any of the wine?"

Persephone smiled brightly. "My word as a goddess."

Peisinoe sighed resignedly. "Well, I don't see the harm in going to see who's over there. And Orpheus plays so beautifully."

Aglaope stared agog while her sisters flanked Persephone and started walking away from the beach. She stood her ground; she was not going to go with them. She knew they were going to drink and dance and party. Let her sisters get in trouble for not doing their jobs if Demeter caught them. Aglaope was already in over her head with Persephone. She dug the claws on her feet into the sand and kicked it out, creating clouds of miniscule glass on the breeze.

*

The ground began to shake beneath her. Instinctually, she leapt to the sky. From her bird's-eye view, Aglaope saw her worst nightmare unfold. The ground opened up some distance away, and her sisters were airborne. Aglaope soared in their direction; as she neared the gash in the earth, she heard screams and watched as nymphs flitted away into the trees and naiads melted into the nearby river.

Aglaope reached Peisinoe first. "What happened? Peisinoe! You need to talk to me!"

Peisinoe looked Aglaope in the eyes and started screaming, "I only had one glass. She said it would be fine. One glass. I have failed. We have failed."

Aglaope flew over to Thelxiepeia, who was weaving heavily in the air. "Thelxiepeia, are you all right?"

Thelxiepeia giggled. "Persephone gave me so much wine. Boy, you missed a party."

"Where is Persephone?"

"With the horses."

Aglaope jerked back as though she had been slapped. "The hors— Oh goddess no!" She tucked her wings in tight against her body and allowed her body to plummet to the black hold below her. Her target was the chariot that was descending with fiery onyx horses in the lead.

Aglaope landed hard on the cold surface of the Under-World, shoved to her feet, and spun around looking for Persephone. She spotted Hades handing her down off the chariot, nothing in his eyes but love for his mistress.

Aglaope raced to where they were, but was blocked by the gates. "Charon! You have to let me through!"

A voice spoke from the gate, "I did warn you, child, that this would all going sideways."

Aglaope screamed and clawed at the gate; all the while, Persephone rushed with Hades to the platter one of his servants had laid out for them. She watched in horror as Persephone ate five pomegranate seeds.

Aglaope sank to the ground and let the sticky mist cling to her skin, her dress. She inhaled deeply, praying for death.

Persephone glided over to the gate and knelt by Aglaope. "You understand, don't you? I had to leave. I had to get down here."

Aglaope shook her head. "This was not the plan. You promised to follow the plan."

Persephone shrugged. "I made a new plan." She stood then, and with a shake of her skirts, Persephone's pure-white dress turned into a dress made of the night sky. Her skin faded to a marble grey, and upon her head, a crown of silver and moonlight. "And this one suits me far better than your safe plan."

*

Marched off.
Forced to stand trial.
For what?
More lies.

*

Aglaope slogged back to the surface. When she came through the rocky wall, the hole was gone, and everything looked as it should. Except her sisters were gone, and Hermes was waiting for her.

Hermes was tricky to deal with; he often played for both sides of the gods, and whichever side was stronger, that was the side he was on. Aglaope rolled her eyes; he was supposed to be impartial, but, really, he was as fickle as the wind.

Hermes's smile stretched thin over two rows of square teeth, and as Aglaope approached, he pointed his caduceus at Aglaope's heart. "You have been summoned."

"I'm sure I have. Where are my sisters?"

Hermes laughed bitterly. "That is why you have been summoned. You are to bear witness to their punishment."

Aglaope's mouth fell open. "Their what?"

"They have failed Demeter, and at Peisinoe's admission, you were the only one to stand against this whole debacle. Not only did you know it was a bad idea, but we have also been informed that you are the only one who went to the UnderWorld at all. Did you try to save your lady?" Hermes directed an oily sneer at Aglaope.

Aglaope felt sick. "Let's go. I have my own words to say to the High Court."

Hermes lifted his scepter and leaned against it casually. "As you wish."

With a roll of thunder, Hermes reached out and grabbed Aglaope around the upper part of her arm. To her credit, Aglaope flinched only a little. "Don't worry. I don't bite," Hermes said as they took to the sky.

The air grew heavier as they neared the court. Aglaope could feel the oppressive anger before they landed lightly, Hermes unceremoniously dropping her on the cloud floor. "I have found the missing sister," he said.

"You are dismissed, messenger," Zeus boomed.

Aglaope looked at the gods before her. Zeus was at the head of the gathering, Hera beside him. To the side of Hera was Poseidon, stroking his kelpy beard, eyebrows pulled low over his eyes. To the side of Zeus was an empty throne of cold lapis and gunmetal agate. That throne had been empty since Hades was banished to the UnderWorld years prior.

And at the feet of Zeus, crumpled in a show of dramatic sobbing—Demeter.

Aglaope stood with her head held high and strode forward. "I demand to see my sisters. And that you release them at once."

The gods all laughed.

Aglaope frowned. "Did you hear me? Take me to my sisters."

Zeus held up a hand, and silence fell. "You have no room to demand anything. Really, this is just a courtesy to ensure we know exactly what happened, so that we can inflict the appropriate punishment on your sisters." He gestured broadly, clouds parted, and there, in an angelically white cage, were Peisinoe and Thelxiepeia.

Peisinoe stood still as a statue, and though Aglaope could see how terrified she truly was, anyone on the outside would only think that she was being defiant. Thelxiepeia was another story. She stalked around the cage like an animal. Every time she touched the bars, lightning shot out and shocked her. She caught Aglaope's eye and, glaring, grabbed hold of the bars and allowed the electricity to shoot through her body, all the while remaining alarmingly silent.

Aglaope looked back at Zeus. "Let. Them. Go. They had nothing to do with this."

Zeus leaned forward. "Oh? And you know who did?"

"You are not going to want to hear this."

"I think we do. Sing for me, Siren. Let us sort this out once and for all."

Aglaope cleared her throat. "For the past several months, I have been hatching a plan with Persephone to help her escape into the UnderWorld. I have passed letters between Persephone and the Lord of the Dead, and back again. Hades was to come to the surface and gather his prize in the coming weeks, and with none of the fanfare that occurred today."

Demeter was on her feet and had Aglaope's hair in her fist in seconds. "Liar! Persephone is my golden girl. She would never betray me this way!" Zeus smiled and let Demeter rail away at Aglaope, watching as Demeter beat her with whips made from wheat stalks.

"Enough!" Aglaope shoved Demeter away. "Bring her here. Bring Persephone forth. She will tell you that is was all her plan, and that my sisters had nothing to do with it."

"That will take time. Time we just don't have. We need to end this now," Zeus said haughtily.

"Milord, shouldn't we hear from young Persephone. It would be a shame to waste our time on half-truths," Hera said from Zeus's side, speaking in a monotone voice without looking up from her lap.

Zeus glared down at his wife, but looked up at the court magnanimously. "Of course, my lovely wife is correct. Let us summon the tiny damned goddess."

Demeter glowered at Aglaope one final time before, covering her face with her hands and with demonstrative flair, she threw herself back on the floor at Zeus's feet.

*

As least I will
Always have my sisters.
While you
Can sleep
Soundly at night
In the bed you made
So tight.

*

While they waited for Hermes to return with Persephone, Aglaope was thrown into the cage with her sisters. After Zeus dropped the cloudy curtain back in front of them, Aglaope collapsed in a moment of relief; it was short-lived, as Peisinoe immediately yanked her to her feet. "You did what?"

"I wanted to help her. She seemed so sad and so sincere. I wanted to help her." It was all Aglaope could say.

"Help her? Help her? We were not serving *her*! We were serving Demeter. You have endangered all of us."

"Yes, I know. She swore you and Thelxiepeia would be safe. She gave her word."

Peisinoe choked on dissonant laughter. "You took the word of a minor goddess? One who has never shown any sign of empathy or depth of feeling for anyone except herself?"

"Yes." Aglaope was tired and needed to save her arguing for when the time came to free her sisters. It would be her death, she knew that, but at least they would be safe.

Time meant nothing in their cloud prison. Aglaope wasn't sure if it had been days or mere moments before the curtain was pulled back. Immediately, though, she knew that trouble was brewing. The once-white High Court was murky grey. Hermes had not only delivered Persephone to court, but her husband as well. While Persephone still wore the dress and crown that Aglaope had watched her transform into, she had made herself look small and hollow.

Aglaope narrowed her eyes at Hades. He was enormous, compared to his brothers. Black hair slicked back, sideburns that flowed down into a new-moon beard. Eyes that had become milky white after the amount of time he'd spent in the depths of the UnderWorld.

Demeter was nowhere to be seen.

Aglaope looked at Zeus, who was leaning as far away from his older brother as his throne would allow. "Bring forth the accused," he said.

The clouds evaporated from around the sisters, and they were pushed forward by Hermes.

"Sirens, you are hereby accused of collusion with my brother, a known criminal of the highest order. If found guilty, you will be sentenced to immediate banishment and death by starvation."

Peisinoe wept silently, and Thelxiepeia growled. Aglaope was only one who spoke. "My lords and my goddesses, I beg of you; let my sisters go. They had nothing do with this scheme. It was purely between Persephone and me."

"So you say. And yet we have heard a very different version from Persephone herself, haven't we?"

Hades yanked on a chain that Aglaope hadn't noticed before, and Persephone, at the end of the chain, stood meekly and looked down at her hands before speaking. "Family, a grave mistake has been made. The Siren sisters spent the time they were supposed to be protecting me making deals with the Lord of the UnderWorld in order to be free of me. You know I wanted nothing more than to please you." She was using her high-pitched child's voice. It grated on Aglaope fiercely. "Now, because I was tricked into eating the fruit of the dead, I must remain Hades's queen for six months of the year. Imagine. All because my guardians were traitors."

"What?" Aglaope could remain silent no longer. "That is not what happened, Persephone. Please tell them. You gave me your word you would not let any harm come to my sisters if I helped you. Please. Tell them."

Hades yanked the chain again, and Persephone sat down. "I think we can all see what's going on here." Hades paused to laugh at his joke. "The Siren sisters are resentful at being unrecognized for their hard work, and so they decided to get rid of the problem. Besides, if it's proof you all need, I'm sure Charon would be more than happy to come up here and show the payments he's been receiving from Aglaope."

"Yes! From me! Just me! My sisters had nothing to do with this!"

Hades trained his empty eyes on Aglaope. "Then tell me about the day I came to claim my prize."

"What? What do you mean?"

"Did you or did you not send them to the Satyrs' picnic?"

"I did, sir."

"Knowing the Satyrs' penchant for enhanced wine?"

Peisinoe stepped forward. "We gave our word we wouldn't have any of the wine, and then Persephone pleaded with us to try just a glass. Told us it would make the music so much fuller. To have a little fun for once."

Poseidon sneered and interjected, "And did you? Have a little fun?"

"Unfortunately, more fun than I can remember." Peisinoe bowed her head.

"May I please say something, husband?" Persephone mewed.

"Of course, my love. And then we will away. It is bright here, and I have a headache."

Persephone nodded. "Family, because I must endure my banishment without complaint, I think it only fair that those involved should also endure. Why are we continuing with this show? Send them away as I have been sent away." Persephone shrank back into herself.

Zeus nodded. "Yes, I also grow weary of this activity. Sirens, you are banished, having brought forth no proof and no clear argument of what actually took place. Neither will you eat that which has been set forth on the sea with protection from Poseidon, nor will you leave the boundaries of your island and small cove. If you do, you will meet with certain death." Zeus snapped a lightning bolt on the ground.

Everyone vanished, except for Hades and Persephone. Persephone stood tall and took the lead as they prepared to depart. Before leaving, she faced the Sirens with a cruel smile on her face. "Charon did warn you. And I told you; I always get what I want." She tugged on the chain, and Hades followed after her with a broad smile on his face.

As soon as they were gone, Hermes appeared. "Let's go see your new home."

NOVA

*T*he door in front of me opened. *"Hey, I'm home."*

"Who's that?" my mom called from the kitchen. I looked away from my younger self to glare at the kitchen. Who else would it be? I'm the only child you had.

"I'll go see." My dad, he could always see me; he just didn't care to.

"It's Nova," my younger self reminded them.

My dad came out of the kitchen. "Oh good, I need to talk to you."

I shook my head. No. Not this one. Can't she just take the memories. I have to relive them first?

"Who's Nova?" my mom called.

I looked back at myself, knowing the crushing blow that came every time she said that. But there was no outward reaction, just a blank countenance. "Sure, Dad. What's up?"

"Let's go for a walk."

I blinked hard. Don't go on that walk. You do not want to hear what he has to say. Stay here. *The more I blinked away the tears, the more dim everything became, until I was standing in an endless nothingness. I spun around.*

I could hear Aggie's voice ebbing away. "No!" *I screamed.* "If you're going to take this one, take the whole thing."

I squeezed my eyes shut and willed the rest of the memory to come forward. "The stone bridge. The rose garden, we stopped there. That's where he—"

"Nova, I need to tell you something. Honestly, I should have told you this a long time ago, and kept telling you your whole life. But it always slipped my mind."

I opened my eyes. There we were, standing on that bridge. That was the last time I ever came to this garden. I wept silently.

"What is it, Dad. I've got homework."

"I know you think your mom and I forget about you…a lot."

"And everyone else. I mean, except Ryan."

My dad waved that away. "Right, and everyone else. But, look, there is a reason. It's because you are from a very powerful magical line. Those who inherit this magic have the greatest gift. Now, I wasn't lucky enough to have gotten it, and maybe I was little bit resentful, but it's not like I left you completely alone."

"I don't understand. Magical line?"

"Right, I've gotten off topic. You're so distracting when you chatter on like that."

"Sorry," my younger self muttered while looking down at their shoes.

My dad shook his head dismissively. "No matter. You're invisible."

Even though I remembered this moment as clear as day and knew what he was about to say, my body still jerked back as though it had been punched. My memory self ran their hands through their hair. "I'm what?"

My dad smiled cruelly. "More than that, you're barely a memory in people's minds. It's amazing. You can do anything! You don't even have to go to school anymore. No one would know."

"I would know. Ryan. Ryan would know."

It was all I could do to face this memory again, the moment when everything became clear…and also fell completely away from me. My whole life, I had been ignored. Forgotten. And why? Because I had inherited some weird magic from my dad. And now he is justifying his neglect? Who the hell does he think he is? To keep this from me? And then to act like just telling me fixes everything?

I stood behind myself on that bridge and watched as I straightened my posture, looked up at my dad, and said, "To hell with you." And my younger self took off. As I watched myself fade into the distance, I let the rest of the world go with it. It was time to let all of this go.

I smiled, and for the first time in my life, I felt at peace.

It was short-lived.

With each exhale, I let go of my hurt, disappointment, and pain. With every inhale, I took in the next layer of Aggie's most deeply held secrets. Her desire to protect her sisters. Her lost innocence at a so-called friend's betrayal. "My sisters had nothing to do with this!" echoed into my ears as visions flew through my head.

Secret visions humans were never meant to see. Monolithic beings that were solid one minute and pure energy the next. Their indifferent anger poured into me until I couldn't bear to look anymore.

I turned my back and came face-to-face with Aggie. Her wings spread wide, the tips of the feathers blending in with the fuzzy grey surrounding us. She was protecting her sisters, but I could already see it was too late.

There was a snap of electricity.

*

My eyes snapped open. *Dammit, I'm tired of this.*

Aggie was perched on a log in front me. Smiling. Something in her had shifted; she seemed lighter somehow. "So you're awake?"

I sat up, and my back creaked under the weight of the secrets I had traded. "Yeah, I guess." I forced myself up straight, but then had to let my back hunch over to ease the pain.

"It's the rocks. They're getting bigger."

"And?" I lifted my head and glared at Aggie.

Aggie shrugged and jumped down from the log. "Probably should have learned to control that power before being around—oh, I don't know—anybody."

"Maybe you should learn to mind your own business."

Aggie walked over and sat down next to me. She bumped my side as if we were good friends, the way Ryan used to before—

"It's a shame."

"What is?"

"That no one is going to miss you."

"For who is it a shame?"

Aggie laughed. "Yeah, I guess you're right. Listen, I need to keep moving. I don't know where my sister is, but I do know that she is gunning for me. Honestly, if it weren't for her insatiable appetite, she would have killed me when she took Ryan."

"Why? Why is she hunting you?"

Aggie looked at her hands. "She's not. Not really. I mean, don't get me wrong; she'll kill me when she gets the chance, but it's our older sister she's really after. Peisinoe...I think she got off the island. I think she's free." Aggie took a deep breath, and her shoulders dropped as she relaxed into herself.

"I'm glad. That she's free. I'm sorry you're not."

Aggie tensed again and looked over at me. "Neither are you." Aggie started to sing.

This time, I let myself slide into the hypnotic trance. Grateful for the end.

2020

Rose's garden is beautiful

But we never, never say that

In the long, dark sky.

*

L ightning ignited the night sky as Rose clawed her way through the inky blackness. With what little magic she had, Rose curled her long fingers toward the sky to seal the cracks. Breath heaving, Rose scanned the darkness for her prey. *There!* Movement to her left caught her eye, and she set off at a run. "You can't hide for long! I will find you!"

Rose stopped suddenly, braced her hands on her hips, and bent forward to catch her breath. She was lost. In her own garden! Another flash of lightning blinded Rose, and as her eyes readjusted to the darkness, she saw that she was in the herb garden. Rose took a moment to try to figure out which herbs could help her, but she was damned if she could remember. At this point, Rose wasn't even sure she could name the herbs that were in front of her. Just one more thing that the Siren had taken from her.

*

Rose plants willows in her garden gold
Lilies, violets, yellow tulips bold
She plants milkweed and chrysanthemum
But she never plants a rose tree
And I don't ask why.

*

The cottage sat in the middle of a riotous bed of flowers. A river bordered one side of the garden, and worn white fencing marked the edges on the other three sides. A small arched gate sat at the end of a small path; its rusted lock had long since broken and no longer kept unwanted visitors out. If such a visitor were to find her gate and walk through it, they would be completely cut off from the real world outside. It was punishment for crimes committed by her and her sister.

The gate creaked open, and Rose snapped to attention. Her eyes narrowed as she looked through the stained-glass window that in the early afternoon sun threw shades of blue and red across her face. Rose saw a tall, blonde woman, hair wildly curling down her back, standing at the garden gate. Rose guessed, based on the long sleeves and threadbare shawl, that it was winter outside, or at the very least, autumn.

Something didn't feel quite right about this one; Rose shrugged off the feeling as she walked to the gate. Pasting a smile on her face, she stepped outside to greet her new guest. As the woman came closer, Rose noticed that her new guest looked otherworldly. Beyond her golden hair, she had clear-porcelain skin and green eyes that were the same pale jade shade as the succulents Rose used to decorate her window boxes.

Still smiling, Rose raised her hand in greeting and waited patiently for her guest to adjust the lute strapped to her back before stepping off her porch to meet her. "Hello there!"

"Good day. I seem to be lost; maybe you can help me find my way back to the trail?" the young woman asked, looking around.

"I could, but might I ask what brings you here?" Rose let her arms hang at her sides, trying to appear relaxed. She didn't want to scare this woman, but she also didn't want to let her guard down. Rose wasn't sure what this woman's secret was, but Rose was sure that her instincts were correct. This woman was bad news.

"I'm not sure. I stopped to rest my feet—I've been walking a long way—and when I stood up, I was at your gate."

Rose nodded and pursed her lips. "Well, it's getting late. Why don't you come inside for the night? I've got soup on for dinner, and I'll make you some tea."

"Thank you. In return for your hospitality, I'll sing for you. I am a traveling musician by trade. My name is Aggie."

"That would be lovely. My name is Rose. Welcome to my garden and my home."

*

While Aggie settled herself in the attic bedroom to which Rose had shown her, Rose stood over the soup pot, putting the finishing touches on the vegetable soup. She fished out a bundle of herbs that included rosemary and lemon balm. She stirred the pot gently, reciting a small spell to encourage rest. Rose had just finished setting the table when Aggie reappeared.

"Wow, that smells incredible." Aggie wasted no time digging into her soup and warm bread.

"Thank you. It's amazing what fresh ingredients can do for a meal."

Aggie held the back of her hand to her mouth to cover it as she said with a full mouth, "Yeah, I saw your garden as we were walking in; it's...extensive."

"After you finish eating, we should go for a walk. Then you can see how extensive it really is."

Aggie was already yawning as she replied, "That sounds great."

Aggie hadn't even finished eating before the magic-infused soup took effect. Grabbing Aggie under the arms, Rose hauled her up and half-dragged, half-carried Aggie up the stairs. Something scratched Rose as she dropped Aggie onto the bed. She rubbed her shoulder as she looked around, trying to figure out what had been so sharp.

Rose squinted when she saw something poking through Aggie's shawl. She bent over Aggie and pulled a taupe feather from the shawl. She held it between two fingers and twirled it slowly. *Too big to belong to a mourning dove.* She crossed both arms over her chest and looked down at her sleeping guest. "Who are you?"

*

Rose plants asters and wisterias
Phlox and sages and veronicas.
She plants irises and daffodils.
But she never plants a rose tree,
And I don't ask why.

*

Rose trampled the herbs; they were useless to her now, anyway. She had to find Aggie; it was time to end this. With every piece of knowledge, every memory that Aggie stole, the magic protecting Rose's garden weakened. Now, all that was left was a garden full of flowers she didn't recognize and a lifetime of emptiness.

SPLASH!

"The river!" Rose turned a sharp left and headed toward the water.

At the bank, Rose tripped over a pair of red, child-sized shoes. She picked them up. *Why do I have these?* Rose never had children, even though she wanted them. *I did?* Rose laughed humorlessly; she didn't even know that anymore. Rose dropped the shoes when she heard splashing downriver.

"There's no way out from the river, my girl. Keep running."

*

Won't you come into my garden green?
Garden perfumed like a world unseen?

Rose, oh, Rosie, won't you marry me?
When I shower her with roses
She begins to cry.

*

"Aggie! Come on sleepyhead! It's time to get up! We don't sleep the day away here!" Rose called up the stairs.

Rose hadn't slept at all the night before. *Where did the feather come from? What bird is big enough to have feathers that large?*

In the predawn twilight, Rose had given up all hope of sleep, gone to her garden, and selected a small bouquet of flowers. It was only as she was tying the flowers with a red ribbon, the feather poised in the front, that she realized what she had picked. Lilacs, forget-me-nots, and red chrysanthemums. Love flowers.

Rose decided it was all coincidence; she had picked these particular blooms because they were pretty, not because she was hopeful. She set the flowers, complete with ribbon and feather, in a small vase at the center of her table. She smiled at them as Aggie stopped at the bottom the stairs.

"Where did you get that?"

Rose looked up at Aggie, and her smile faded. "What's wrong?"

"The feather. Where did you get it?"

Rose shrugged and said, "It was stuck in your shawl last night. I was worried it would scratch you, like it did me when I walked you to your bed."

Aggie rubbed her arms. "Oh, thank you."

Rose pushed away the nagging feeling that something was wrong. "It's fine. Would you like some breakfast? I have some fruit I could cut for you."

Aggie slowly walked to the table and sat down. "I'm fine. I'm sorry I fell asleep at your table last night. You should have just left me here."

"Don't be silly." Rose waved Aggie's statement away. "You told me yourself that you had been walking for a long way. Warm food always makes me groggy too."

Aggie nodded and looked around. "I would pay you with a song right now if I could find my lute."

"I put it away for you. It's by the front door. You can play for me later."

Aggie ran her hands through her hair nervously and tried to comb out the snarls with her fingers. "Um, do you have a comb or a brush I could use?"

Rose smiled and walked to a cabinet. "I sure do." She pulled a golden comb from the top shelf and moved behind Aggie. Slowly, she started to run the comb through Aggie's long tresses.

"You don't have to do that,"

Rose smiled darkly. "Oh, but I do." Secrets or no, Aggie was meant to be her companion. *Let's hope she lasts longer than the others.* Rose looked out the kitchen window to a far point in the garden. *I would hate to lose another.*

Aggie started to relax, and eventually to doze again.

As Rose rhythmically ran the comb through her hair, she could feel the effects of the comb taking hold. Soon, there would be nothing in Aggie's heart and soul but Rose. They could be together, and this time there would be no mistakes. In the past, there had been companions whom Rose had loved, but she left clues about because she had been careless. When her companions remembered who they were, Rose couldn't let them go. They had all promised to stay with her forever, and so they did.

Except one. She thought about the red shoes that stood guard at the river's edge. Gerta was the only one who got away.

Rose gripped the comb tightly and pulled too harshly.

"Ouch! Rose, please, I'm a tad tender headed."

Rose looked down at Aggie's upturned face and smiled gently. "I'm sorry. I was woolgathering. How about we go for a walk?"

*

It wasn't long before Rose and Aggie fell into a routine. Every morning, Rose combed through Aggie's hair while they planned their day—a walk through the garden while Rose taught Aggie about the flowers and herbs she grew, or Aggie trying to teach Rose how to weave on the loom that Aggie found in the corner of the attic covered in dust. Some days, they just sat on the porch in silence. Every day was a perfect summer day—piercing-blue skies, gentle breezes that tickled noses with an abundance of fragrances, and always a pitcherful of fresh lemonade or iced tea within arm's reach.

Rose was happy. Borderline delirious. Aggie was perfect in every way. Rose made sure that Aggie stayed that way by brushing her hair every morning. It not only kept Aggie agreeable, but also kept the memory charm in place. It was all going so well that Rose didn't see the other shoe getting ready to drop until it was too late.

"Why are there no roses?"

Rose stopped midstride and brought Aggie to a halt with her. "Excuse me?"

"Roses. We have no roses. We have every other flower known to man in this garden, and yet there aren't any roses."

"Well"—Rose gestured impatiently—"they're just so *pedestrian*, aren't they?"

"I wouldn't say that."

"Well, I would," Rose replied too harshly. She didn't keep roses, not since Gerta. That little girl had crushed her, called her names, and when Rose had tried to stop her from leaving to bring their magic back, she had escaped. The night Gerta got away, barefoot and bleeding, Rose had ripped every rosebush from the garden and burned them. The smell of burning roses was seared in her memory.

"I'm sorry. I didn't mean to upset you."

"No, I'm sorry. We should head back to the house. I'm getting tired."

That night while Aggie slept, Rose made sure that the lute was locked away. She knew that she should destroy it, that it would break the hold that she had on Aggie. Yet, just as she had with every other one of her companions, Rose wanted to keep something of Aggie's. Something tangible.

When the night was quiet, and Rose was sure that Aggie was sleeping, she unlocked her closet, took out the lute, and held it in her hands. Sitting on the edge of her bed, feeling the weight in her hands and on her lap, Rose wondered about the music it played, the joy it brought people.

That was the downside to erasing people's memories; Rose was never able to learn about why people traveled with certain things. The mementos that Rose kept didn't tell her anything about who these people were. Rose reluctantly set the lute back in the closet and clicked the lock into place.

Aggie was the biggest mystery of all. She had so much knowledge and was so eager to learn more. She was voracious on their walks, when they talked about the flowers, why some flowers had to be kept in boxes, and why others could run rampant in the fields. Aggie couldn't get enough. Though, lately their walks were being cut short because Aggie claimed she needed to lie down. Maybe Aggie was getting bored.

Rose shook her head as she climbed into bed; she would figure it out in the morning.

*

The next morning, Aggie did not get up, even after Rose's usual prodding. Rose walked up to the attic, and upon spying Aggie still in bed, noticed that Aggie had grown sickly thin. She was always wearing that cloak; it had hidden the weight loss. But in bed, under only a nightshirt and cotton sheet, it was obvious. The outline of Aggie's body was so shrunken that Rose was completely taken aback.

What is happening? Aggie eats every meal, doesn't she? Rose thought back over their time together, but she had been so taken with her new companion that she hadn't paid attention.

Rose pulled the sheet back and brushed her hands over Aggie's bony shoulders, down her arms. As Rose's fingers ran around the hem of the sleeve, she felt something. *Feathers?* Gently, she lifted the sleeve and peered down. Running the length of Aggie's upper arm and to her shoulder were dove-grey feathers similar to the one she had pulled from Aggie's cloak that first night.

Rose was so focused that she didn't see that Aggie had woken up and was staring, horrified, up at her. "What are you doing up here?"

Rose jerked back. "I'm sorry. You didn't come down, and I called up, but..." Rose looked away.

"I'm not feeling well. I'm sorry if that doesn't play into your plans for our day."

Rose looked into Aggie's sharp-boned face. "I'm sorry that you don't feel well, but you don't need to be snide. Why don't I make us some breakfast?"

Aggie shook her head. "No, thank you."

Rose turned and headed back for the stairs. "I'll let you rest. I'll be up in a while to check on you."

Rose paused on the stairs and stole one more look at Aggie; she then turned her face toward the window and closed her eyes. Rose walked out of the cottage and headed toward the river. When she reached the river, she looked once at the red shoes and then headed upriver along the bank.

When she reached the phlox and iris blooms, she turned away from the river and walked into death. There were no flowers here; nothing lived here except memories of those who had come before. The memories she held in her heart were reflected in the cairns she'd built. The piles of stones were stacked with care, and each one held a place in her heart.

Rose sat in the middle of the stone stacks and closed her eyes. Aggie was not all right. She was never hungry, yet it was clear from how gaunt she had become that Aggie was starving. She had feathers running the length of her arms. There were a handful of magical creatures that Aggie could be, but Rose wouldn't be sure until she confronted her. Rose pulled her hair over her shoulder and absently braided it while she considered the possibilities.

*

Rose's garden is beautiful,
But we never, never say that
In the long, dark sky.

*

Rose ran blindly into the darkness, away from the river. She was following Aggie's footsteps and gaining on her. Rose skidded to a halt when she was blinded once again by the lightning. In front of her were piles of stones; they looked as though they were placed intentionally, but Rose couldn't be sure.

And there, in the center of the rock garden, was Aggie. Her hair a tangled mess, eyes bright with fear, and breathing heaving.

"You can't get away!" Rose shouted.

"I'm never going to stop trying. I know what you've been doing here. I know what *this* garden is."

"What is it, then? What is any of this? Why don't I remember?"

"I took your memories. Ate them." Her mouth twisted into a terrible smile. "You were delicious."

Rose screamed and lunged at Aggie, snagging her hair and yanking her to the ground. "You stole from me! I gave you everything!"

Aggie pushed her head against Rose's hand to keep from being pressed fully into the ground. "What about all these other people? Did you give them everything too? What about Gerta? She ran too! The only one who escaped. If you give these people everything, then why do they keep trying to get away?"

Rose stood and kicked Aggie in the ribs. "I wouldn't know. You took those memories from me!"

Trying to catch her breath, Aggie crawled through the rock stacks. "You're absolutely right. I did. And I don't regret it."

Rose growled low. "You will."

Aggie pushed herself to her feet and looked around. "Rose, the magic that you have on this place is breaking. And the more I take, the weaker your magic gets. I wrote you a song, you know."

Aggie took a deep breath and started to sing, praying that it was enough to win her freedom.

*

Now she walks the flowered dark alone.
Black-eyed Susans keeps her company.
Coralbells and hostas cling to her,
And she never plants a rose tree
'Neath the long, dark sky.

*

Rose got back to the cottage and found Aggie sitting on the porch. She couldn't believe that she had missed how sick Aggie had gotten; it was so obvious now.

"So you're back," Aggie said.

Rose nodded, sat in the chair opposite Aggie, and started to rock. "I'm back. I'm really worried about you."

"Why? I'm up, aren't I? Isn't that what you wanted?"

Rose bit back frustration. "I want you feeling better, and I don't know how to help you." Then Rose took a leap of faith. "I'm not even sure what your kind eat."

"My kind?"

"Harpies?"

Aggie sat forward in her chair, eyes narrowed to slits. "No, I don't like that. I am not a Harpy."

"So, you're a Siren?"

Weak, Aggie sagged back in her chair. "It would explain the feathers."

"You're not sure?"

"I haven't been sure of anything since I got here. I walked through that gate, and you became everything."

"The way it should be once you're here."

"I won't survive much longer. I need food."

Rose nodded. "Well, I have an idea. But if you agree to it, you'll also be agreeing to stay here with me."

Aggie turned her head toward Rose. "What?"

"There is a river that crosses the realms. You can go down there and lure river fishermen to you. Eat them, and then come back to me."

"I suppose that's as good a plan as any. I am going to need help getting to the river this time."

Rose stood and offered her hand to Aggie. She pulled Aggie to her feet and steadied her.

Slowly, they walked to the river. Rose filled the silence with stories about the different flowers, trying to ignore how light and fragile Aggie felt in her arms as Aggie rested her head on Rose's shoulder and sighed deeply.

After several minutes, they reached the river. Rose helped Aggie sit on the river's edge. "I'll wait just out of sight for this one time. Just in case no one comes when you call."

Aggie nodded and opened her mouth. While she didn't consciously remember anything that came before being with Rose, her heart did.

Rose could feel the music in her bones, and something pulled at her.

*

Rose regained consciousness, and Aggie was gone. She looked around the riverbank and grew fearful that Aggie had broken her word and found a way out. When there was no trace of Aggie near the water, Rose walked back to the cottage. She stopped for a moment when she heard loud crashing coming from inside.

Rose ran to the open door and saw Aggie pulling door after door off their hinges. "What are you doing?"

"My lute! It's in one of these closets! I saw it! I saw everything!"

"What? Aggie, what's happening?"

Aggie turned and glared at Rose. "What's happening is I am going to find my lute, and then I'm going to leave. You do not get to keep me anymore."

"How do—"

"How do I know? I just do. Now, which closet is my lute in?" Aggie burst into Rose's bedroom. There, in the closet, was Aggie's lute.

Rose leaned in the door and crossed her arms over her chest. "So you have your lute. How do you plan to leave?"

"The way I came. Through the gate."

Rose nodded. "Well, then, be my guest."

Rose followed Aggie out and watched her march down the garden path and try to open the gate. It was shut fast. Rose wore a self-satisfied smile as she watched Aggie shake the gate with all of her strength until she screamed and fell to her knees. Rose didn't move from the front doorway until Aggie came skulking back with her head hung low.

"You're mine. Forever. Let's just put today behind us and be friends again. It's all I ever wanted."

"You don't know what you've done. I will be leaving, whether you let me or not." Aggie stormed into the cottage and up to the attic room.

*

Aggie woke up before sunrise the next morning. She sat at the kitchen table, tuning her lute and waiting. When Rose appeared, Aggie immediately started to strum and hum a wordless tune. Rose staggered forward and braced her hand on the edge of the table. "No. Not this time," Aggie said as she continued to play the lute. When Rose fell to her knees and started mumbling to herself, Aggie sang louder and with greater intent.

Rose braced her hands on her knees and continued reciting the ward. One of the strings on the lute snapped and caught Aggie across the palm of the hand with which she was strumming. Rose wiped the sweat from her brow while Aggie wrapped her hand in a towel.

Aggie leaned against the counter, putting pressure on her cut. "You pack a punch."

Rose straightened her spine and stood erect. "I just want companionship. You have no idea how lonely it is."

"I know more than you think, but you can't keep me here against my will."

"Here, why don't we sit and talk about this over some tea."

Aggie nodded and sat. She watched Rose wander the kitchen for a few minutes before innocently asking, "Do you need some help?"

Rose slammed a cabinet door shut. "No, I don't need help finding my way around my own kitchen!"

Aggie held up her hands. "Okay. Sorry, I won't offer again."

Rose continued to tear through her kitchen until she finally gave up. "I don't want tea. I need to go lie down."

Aggie smiled. "Yeah, I'll bet."

Rose slammed her bedroom door, and Aggie leaned back in the chair. This one was going to be tricky.

*

Over the next several days, Rose lost more of her memory. She found herself wandering the gardens and getting lost; she couldn't remember how to keep apples from browning when she made pie, and when she visited her cairns, she couldn't remember whom they represented, or why she'd chosen certain stones for certain stacks, but not for others. When she went there the day before to escape the cat-and-mouse tension in her cottage, she sobbed when she saw all of the cairns but could only remember two or three of the people to whom they were dedicated.

Worse than anything, she could feel the magic cracking. All of her energy had to be poured into keeping the garden closed. It was exhausting, and something had to be done. Rose laughed to herself; she knew exactly what needed to be done. She should have handled it the moment she realized she had a Siren on her hands, but she had thought that they could still be together.

And this time it could have been forever. She even gave Aggie a way to lure people to her so she could eat them. But what did Aggie do instead? She betrayed Ruth and was chipping away at this haven Rose built.

It was time to end it.

*

Rose's garden is beautiful,
But we never, never say that
In the long, dark sky.
Rose's garden is beautiful,
But we never, never, never, never say that
In the long, dark sky.
—C.S.E. Cooney

*

Aggie's voice quieted as she watched the magic dissolve around her. It fell like rain, leaving only Rose's cottage and a dead garden. Rose lay on the ground, writhing and sobbing. Aggie looked down at her pitifully. "You could have let me go."

Aggie walked back toward the cottage, marveling at how little was left, now that the magic was gone. The cottage was dilapidated and parts of it were rotting. The stained glass that had framed the front door was gone, and in its place were empty frames and threadbare curtains.

Aggie stepped inside, looking only for her cloak and lute. Once she had those, she walked to the gate. It was still stuck fast, but instead of being locked by magic, weeds and grass held it in place. Aggie lifted one booted foot and kicked the gate until it opened.

Screams filled the night behind her as Aggie began her trek west.

Nova

"Ah, the NoWhere." This was bliss. There was no weight, no pain. Just nothing. I smiled. I could still hear Aggie singing and felt the secrets of the song flow into me. "With any luck, this is the last one and then...oblivion."

I closed my eyes and felt the pain of the garden flow through me. Then, on top of the singing, I started hearing the echoes. All around me, voices upon voices. Some were voices I didn't recognize, but secrets I did. Some were voices I recognized, but wished I didn't. It was so exhausting carrying those secrets, and now I wouldn't have to anymore.

"Don't be so sure."

My eyes popped open, and Aggie stood in front of me. But this Aggie was wholly herself—wings spread wide, long legs that flowed down into those of a bird, and arms held above her head.

"You know, one of the gifts of being around for so long is that I catch on really quick to how to use new magic. Ryan's magic is something for the ages. In here, I can be myself again. I can appear to you...to anyone...and give and take whatever I want. I am in control."

My stomach hit my knees, and my face went clammy. "Yes, you've proven that. Time and again. I am not questioning that."

Aggie lowered her arms, and her wings folded in; she strutted over to me. "No, you're not. But you also have started to believe that your end is coming. It's not. Not for a long time. You see, I'm the only one who can see you. Who knows that you are real, and not some figment."

I shook my head. "No. Please."

Aggie cupped my face in her hands. "You have your wish. Oblivion."

*

Night.

It was night.

In the woods.

I'm in the woods.

Alone. I am alone.

I started running. Fingers of branches reached out and grabbed my shirt. Pulled at me. Kept me from moving forward. I *had* to keep moving forward.

I fell. My hands scraped the dirt in front of me. "Where are my hands!?" I screamed. "I can't see my hands!"

I pushed myself up, standing, and felt an enormous weight pulling me down until I was staring at the ground again. "Where is my body?"

I tried to stand up straight, and a hot poker of pain shot through my spine; I had to curve my spine to alleviate it. I continued moving forward, but slower. I was limping under the invisible weight I was carrying, but the slower

I moved, it felt as though the trees and other plants made way for me.

I passed the orange glow of dying fires. I wanted to stop, but as I breathed in the remains of the smoke, visions filled my head. And with every vision, I felt myself pulled farther down. The visions were of people I didn't recognize.

A child eating a cookie.

A woman buying a purse.

Someone opening a hotel-room door.

It wasn't the visions that pulled me down; it was the shame and secrecy I felt in them. I didn't understand what I was seeing. What I was feeling. It was so confusing and painful. I kept pushing forward. I kept my eyes down, willing myself to ignore the possibility of those out there who could help me. But I if I couldn't see myself, how could anyone else see me?

My pace slowed to a crawl. My feet dragged with despair until I broke through the woods…and into civilization.

"A road!" Salvation!

I looked both ways and saw the red glow of the sun breaking over the horizon. I turned in that direction and started walking.

Eventually, I came to a gas station. I squinted up at it; something felt familiar, but I couldn't put my finger on it. When I got to the doors, they were locked. *Dammit.* I leaned against the wall next to the door and slid down to the ground. I let my head fall forward and unconsciousness take me.

TURNING A BLIND EYE
AN INTERLUDE

T he bell jingled over the door of the gas station's convenience store. Gus looked up from his newspaper to greet the new customer. He didn't see anyone, but he could hear them moving around.

"Hello?"

"I'm fine. Everything's *fine,"* a voice called from an aisle that was out of his line of sight.

"Okay, well, let me know if you need any help." Gus shrugged and went back to his paper. With half an ear on his customer, Gus continued to read the paper until an armload of snacks fell on the counter in front of him. His smile faded when he looked up.

"Is this some kind of a joke?"

"I'm starving, and I'll be buying all of these. I don't see what the joke is."

Gus looked around. "Where are you?"

"Dammit, I need you to look harder. I'm right here. Please, can I pay you for these and be on my way?"

Gus pushed away from the counter. *This magic is wrong.* He squinted, and a dirty blur appeared in front of him. *All wrong.* "No, you'll leave, and you'll take your sick sense of humor with you."

"My what?" The voice sounded angry now.

Gus's eyes shifted back and forth. "I don't know what happened to you, but you need to leave."

"Fine. Jeez, I'm starving, and I'm lost, and the first person I talk to, an actual woodland deity, can't even see me."

Gus started. He hadn't been recognized for centuries. *How do they know?*

The voice walked away from him. Gus watched the door open. It remained open for several seconds, and then a bloodcurdling scream filled his shop.

"Why can't I see myself? Why can I see everything else? Why won't anyone help me?"

The bell jingled again as the door shut, and Gus heard sobbing. He stood heavily and lumbered to the door, leaning on his walking stick. He had to look hard, but there it was. That dirty smudge in the air, and the sobbing continued.

Gus walked toward the sound and called out, "Hey! How do you know what I am?"

"What?"

"You called me out. You can't just do that."

"Your secret truth takes up all the space in your little store. I don't know how others haven't seen it."

"Will you tell anyone?"

"Your secret is safe with me." The voice heaved a sigh, and Gus heard slow footsteps walking away.

Rubbing a hand over his face, Gus wearily exhaled and shakily made his way back to his stool behind the counter.

EPILOGUE

The shriek stopped Aggie in her tracks. Aggie thought back to that last sunset on the island. She had been so sure that her younger sister would come with her. That they would take on the world of men together. They would take back everything that had been taken from them…and then some.

How wrong she had been. Thelxiepeia had been so full of hatred and betrayal that it had eaten her soul. Aggie was sorry for that.

Aggie found the parking area she was looking for, and there was the bright-orange Jeep—her ticket out of there, and fast. She'd been walking for so long that this opportunity was too fortuitous to pass up. Aggie cautiously walked up to the Jeep and looked around. There in the driver's seat were the keys that she and Ryan had found on the forest floor.

"Too easy."

She threw her meager belongings into the back and climbed into the driver's seat. Aggie took a moment to appreciate the Jeep's openness. The doors and top had been taken off, and as Aggie drove away from the trails, she tilted her head back and breathed in the clean Pacific Northwest air and let the sun warm her face.

Aggie left the woods and hit the main road with a bump. She drove for a few miles before pulling onto the shoulder to check her map. After studying the map for a little while, Aggie got out. She stood next to the Jeep and looked down the road. She shielded her eyes from the blinding sun and took a deep breath...and choked on the smell that filled her nostrils.

"No."

She turned her eyes skyward. There, in the distance, something was flying toward the mountains.

"Hades and damnation."

Aggie piled back into the Jeep, whipped onto the road, and drove off.

*

Aggie zigzagged around for hours, trying to escape the smell of pure rage that was following her; finally, she decided that it was no use, and she pulled off at a sign that advertised a trading post. In a cloud of dust, she pulled into the poor excuse for a parking lot, gathered all of the items she had collected over the past few days, and walked into the trading post.

After Aggie dropped all the camping supplies she didn't need on the table in the trading post, the man working the counter told her to take a look around and scoop up anything she needed.

"I'm sorry. I'm in a hurry. I don't need anything right now."

"But this is a trading post. Not a dropping-off post." The man smiled at his little joke.

Aggie just smiled and told him breathlessly, "I guess it's your lucky day." She yanked the keys out of her pocket, ran to the Jeep, piled into the driver's seat, and drove away.

*

Thelxiepeia landed a short distance from the trading post and closed the distance on foot. Inside the trading post, she stared at all the stuff that was spread on the different tables.

She was grimacing when a woman came from the back and asked, "Is there anything I can help you with?"

"I need things." Her voice was rough, as though she were speaking with a mouthful of gravel.

The sound startled the proprietor of the post, and she took a small step back to put more distance between her and the newcomer. "I see, well, we have plenty of…things. Would you like some water?"

"Yes."

She reached out, holding a water bottle with the tips of her fingers. "Here you go. My name is Tabby. If you have any questions, I'll be right over there."

"Fine."

Tabby was taken aback by Thelxiepeia's brusque tone, but let it go. She decided to keep an eye on her; if she needed to, Tabby would call the police. Tabby took her place behind the counter and kept a discreet eye on her customer.

Shortly, her husband joined her. "Everything okay?"

Thelxiepeia spoke up, "Actually, no, it isn't."

"Oh?"

Thelxiepeia shoved her hair out of her face and then held up a sleeping bag that she had been sniffing. "Where did you get this?"

"A young woman just dropped that off. You actually look a lot like her, although she wasn't as tan as you. We have sunscreen if you would like. Skin cancer is a real killer." He shook his head. "Sorry, I got off topic. Anyway, she didn't even want anything in return. I guess she didn't understand that we're a trading post, not a dropping-off post." The man laughed again at his little joke and was disappointed when it didn't even get a smile this time.

"Pete, I don't think we should be joking right now," Tabby whispered to her husband while she watched the woman's eyes narrow.

Pete cleared his throat. "Sorry, bad joke."

"Did that *woman* drop anything else off?"

Tabby gestured and replied, "Everything on that table."

Thelxiepeia leaned over the table and sniffed everything. "I knew it. I knew she was here."

Pete started to get nervous; he nudged his wife, and she nodded. Tabby grabbed her phone and dialed 911. "I think it's time for you to leave now."

Thelxiepeia clenched her fists at her sides. "I'll leave when I'm finished." Her wings unfurled.

As Tabby whispered into the phone, Thelxiepeia flew across the counter, yanked the woman's arm off, and threw it to the floor. "I *said* I'll leave when I'm finished."

Tabby collapsed, but Pete didn't even have time to react or even scream before Thelxiepeia's black talons sank into his throat. Tabby screamed as she watched from the ground as her husband was covered by the killer's wings.

Once Thelxiepeia was finished with Pete, she turned her sights on Tabby.

*

When the police arrived, all they found was carnage. There were no witnesses, and no one had been left alive. As they were leaving the scene, one of the officers said, "This is just like those other deaths that I heard about on the news this morning."

His partner agreed, "Yup, we'll let the captain know." They rode back to the station silently, both happy that this case would have to be handled farther up the chain.

*

The sun was setting behind Aggie when the shadow fell across the Jeep. She slowed and looked up through the open roof. What she saw chilled her to the core. Aggie pulled onto the shoulder and took several deep breaths before she got out of the Jeep.

"Aglaope, I told your friend to tell you I was coming back for you."

"Well, you've found me."

Thelxiepeia bared her teeth. "It's time for you to come home."

ENDNOTE

The story Gerta tells her grandchildren at the beginning of "1890" is loosely based on "The Snow Queen," a famous short story written by Hans Christian Andersen.